The Wretched Wreath Seller's Christmas Miracle

Nell Harte

©Copyright 2021 Nell Harte

All Rights Reserved

License Notes

This Book is licensed for personal enjoyment only. It may not be resold. No part of this work may be reproduced in any form or by any electronic or mechanical means including information storage and retrieval systems, without written permission from the author

Disclaimer

This story is a work of fiction, any resemblance to people is purely coincidence. All places, names, events, businesses, etc. are used in a fictional manner. All characters are from the imagination of the author.

Table of Contents

Would you like a free book? vii

Chapter One 1

Chapter Two 15

Chapter Three 27

Chapter Four 39

Chapter Five 47

Chapter Six 51

Chapter Seven 67

Chapter Eight 85

Chapter Nine 101

Chapter Ten 115

Chapter Eleven 127

Chapter Twelve 141

Chapter Thirteen 161

Chapter Fourteen 175

Epilogue 191

Join my Newsletter 195

Would you like a free book?

Claim The Beggar Urchins Here by clicking here

Chapter One

1875, London

Edith Atkinson took a deep breath, trying to stay patient with the small child who faced her over the rickety kitchen table. The little boy held out a tin plate, which bore a greyish blob of cold, sticky gruel.

"But why not?" he was demanding, his eyes wide and soft.

Little Benny Arker's clothes had never yet been mended. He hadn't been coming to the dame school for very long, and Edith could guess that it hadn't been long since his family had moved to their street, either. They must have lived somewhere better before then, somewhere that a seven-year-old boy didn't grow up knowing why he couldn't have more than she'd given him.

"Because otherwise there won't be enough to go around, Benny," said Edith. A headache pounded at her temples; she tried to ignore it, forcing a smile.

"This pot is all we have, see? And we have to share it around nicely between everyone."

"All we have?" said Benny, his eyes resting on the tin pot that stood on the little coal stove.

"That's right. So run along and eat your tea, now," said Edith. "Before it goes cold."

Benny looked at her with confusion for a few moments longer. She could sense the questions buzzing around his head, and remembered how she'd wanted to ask those same questions four years ago when she was about Benny's age. About why there suddenly just wasn't enough. About how it was possible to be this hungry.

To her relief, though, Benny drifted away, and Edith turned back to the pot to ladle out another spoonful of gruel. She plopped it onto a plate with a wet splat, then turned to hand it to the next child over the table.

A few spoonfuls later, the pot was all but empty, and there was still one child left.

Tiny Donna Walsh, a mere little scrap of a thing, with great dark eyes that seemed to hold all the secrets of the universe within their depths.

Edith smiled at the five-year-old despite her exhaustion. "Just a second, love," she said, her stomach clenching as she turned back to the pot of gruel.

She'd hoped there would be a little left over for her, but she knew what Mama would say if she skimped on any of the children's meals. She'd said it so often when Edith was younger: "We still have a bit of bread or fish for supper, Edie, but some of these poor things will go home to nothing."

Edith suspected that Donna Walsh was one of the children who went to bed hungry. With a mammoth effort, she scraped and scraped at the pot until every last scrap of gruel was on the tin plate. "Here you are, Donna," she said, handing the plate to the tiny girl.

"Thank you very much, Miss Edith," said Donna, with exquisite politeness, as children always learned here.

Edith watched as the children settled themselves down, sitting on the bare stone of the little courtyard outside the back door.

They sat very still and ate in silence, swallowing the food in great gulps, almost inhaling more than eating. Edith knew that in a matter of seconds, the food would be all gone.

Soft footsteps sounded on the hallway, and Mama came in from the classroom, wiping her hands on her apron to shake off the chalk dust. "Oh, thank you, dear Edie," she said, coming over to Edith and wrapping her arms around her. These days, Mama had to stand on tiptoe to kiss the top of Edith's head. "Is everyone behaving?"

"They're being very good children, Mama," said Edith. "Everyone waited in line nicely and no one is pushing or jostling."

"That's wonderful." Mama draped an arm around Edith's shoulders, and for a few moments they gazed through the open back door, watching the children eat. Edith could feel the bony edges of Mama's ribs against her.

She wished she had thought to try to keep some gruel for Mama, but how could she? There had hardly been enough for the children.

She tipped her head back, leaning it on Mama's arm, and looked up into her mother's face for a few moments.

Mama must have been ravishingly pretty once.

There was something aristocratic about the way her nose tilted upwards at the end, and she had a wide, upturned mouth that seemed to permanently highlight the dimples on her cheeks – deep curves that echoed her every smile. There were crinkles around her eyes now, and her cheeks were a little hollow, the high cheekbones standing out a little more than they really should. Streaks of grey made her golden hair look faded underneath her patched and tired headscarf, the ends of which drooped over her shoulders like the ears of a sorrowful hound.

"Mama?" said Edith.

"Yes, poppet?"

Edith leaned a little closer to her. "Can't we give the children just a little more gruel?" she asked, trying to keep her tone from getting too pleading. "Just a little bit more. Benny asked for more, and I couldn't give him any. And Donna... well, she never asks, but I can always tell how very hungry she is."

Mama squeezed Edith gently. "I love you for asking that, my dear. But I'm afraid we can't." She kissed the side of Edith's head. "You know that we can't. We just don't have enough money for everything."

"Then they should pay us more, so that we can feed the children more," said Edith, frustrated.

"It's not as simple as that. Most of the parents are already doing the best that they can." Mama sighed. "We're doing our best, my sweet."

"I know that." Edith cuddled a little closer under her mother's arm.

The children had already finished their tea; they were filtering back into the house now, carrying their empty plates. Timmy and Vicky were on kitchen duty for the day, and normally they were two little chatterboxes. Today, though, there was silence in the kitchen as they started to gather everyone's plates for washing.

"They're quiet today," Mama murmured, for Edith's ears alone. "It's the winter. It makes them tired and sad."

A small wrinkle appeared between Mama's eyebrows. It meant that she was coming up with a solution, and Edith always loved Mama's solutions. After a few seconds, Mama strode forward, putting a hand on Timmy's shoulder.

"Edith and I will help you with the dishes, Tim. We've finished cleaning the classroom and getting ready for tomorrow morning's lessons."

Edith knew that this wasn't strictly true. Mama would be sitting up late tonight, planning her lessons, but she could tell that the children needed some help today.

She was smiling as she stacked the plates on the kitchen table. "Tell me, little Donna," she said, "do you know what's going to happen in just one month's time?"

Donna's head immediately snapped up from where she'd been staring at her bare toes, and a wide smile transfixed the little girl's face, her huge eyes sparkling. "Christmas! Christmas!" she said. "It's just a month left before Christmas!"

"That's quite right." Mama laughed. "Are you excited?"

"I love Christmas," said Donna. "I love the pretty candles and the decorations in the shop windows."

"I love Christmas, too," said Mama. "It's my favourite time of the year. How about you, Edie?"

A flutter of excitement filled Edith's stomach. "I love making decorations!" she said. "And the pretty holly and mistletoe we put everywhere, and making paper chains and cards with all of you. It's so much fun!"

"Sometimes we get special treats on Christmas, too," said Mama. "Don't you, Timmy?"

Timmy's morose expression brightened a little. "Sometimes we'll get a whole roast chicken to share," he said. "If Papa's work is feeling generous."

"We get oranges every Christmas. They're so sweet and delicious," Vicky chimed in.

"How about you, Donna?" asked Edith.

Donna's face fell. "Papa doesn't believe in Christmas," she said softly.

"That's a great pity, my dear, for it would do him a lot of good if he did." Mama smiled. "Did you all know that Christmas is magical?"

"Magical?" Donna's eyes grew huge and deep.

"Yes." Mama laughed. "It gives us hope at the darkest time of the year – hope of something new, freedom, light, and peace."

She scooped Donna into her arms and planted a kiss on the little girl's forehead. "Look at what it's done to this room full of children already. Why, you were all very cross when you came in, but now you're all smiles. If that's not magic, I don't know what is."

With all of her heart, Edith believed what Mama was saying. She knew that the magic was real, because she could see it shining in Mama's eyes, hear it bubbling through the golden tones of her voice. And she just couldn't wait for that most magical time of the year.

~ ~ ~ ~ ~

By the time darkness fell, almost all of the children had gone home. Only little Donna Walsh was left, sitting in front of the coal stove and playing quietly with her only treasure in the world: a tiny doll made of rags.

It was a pitiful thing, its head made of a ball of rags with an extra rag pulled over it, tied at the neck with a bit of string so that the end of the rag flared out to make its dress.

It had had straw hair once, but this had all been loved away; and Edith had often had to redraw the little face with a charcoal stick.

Still, Donna loved it, and she was playing happily with it while Edith finished the last chores of sweeping out the kitchen and setting out the tin cups for the children's breakfast of tea and a rusk.

Donna yawned, politely putting a hand in front of her mouth; Mama put great emphasis on good manners. "When is James coming?" she asked.

"It won't be long, dear," said Mama, who was wiping down the kitchen table. "I'm sure he'll be here any minute."

As if in response to her words, there was a soft rat-tat at the back door. "That'll be James. I'll walk you out," said Edith hastily, setting down her broom.

Mama gave Edith a knowing glance, and a stifled smile danced on her lips. Edith ignored it, despite the way her cheeks burned at the sight.

She held out a hand to Donna, who took it, and led her up to the back door.

The boy standing in the back courtyard was little more than a scarecrow, but there was no part of James Walsh that Edith didn't find endearing.

From the crazy mop of his straw-coloured hair to his too-big feet, stuffed into old boots that gaped at the front to show glimpses of his bare toes, everything about him was gentle.

He held out big hands to his sister with a cry of joy the moment he saw her; Donna rushed into his arms, and James scooped her against his chest, holding her tightly.

"Have you been a good girl today, then?" he asked her, kissing her forehead.

"Yes," said Donna.

"She has." Edith smiled, and James' eyes lifted to hers. They were so much like Donna's, but there was a hint of steel in them; a spark of something fiercely protective that made Edith's spine tingle in a strange way she'd never felt before. She didn't know why James made her feel this way, but she liked it.

"Thank you for taking such good care of her." James lowered Donna to the ground, keeping a firm grip on her hand. "I'm sorry I'm so late again. The costermonger had late customers, and of course I couldn't go until they'd been served."

"I know he drives you hard," said Edith.

James shrugged. "It's honest work, and I'm very glad of it."

He squeezed Donna's hand. "Besides, it's a busy time of the year, which is always a good thing. It won't be long before all the Christmas shopping starts." He winked down at Donna. "And this time, you're not allowed to guess what your present will be, all right?"

Donna gave a delighted giggle. "I will, though," she said. "I will! But you're not allowed to guess, either."

Edith smiled at them. Last year, James' gift to Donna had been one single sticky bun.

She wasn't sure how he had afforded it, but Donna had talked about it for weeks afterwards. She could see strain in his eyes now, but his smile stayed in place.

"Timmy's family gets a roast chicken for Christmas. I've never had a roast chicken before," said Donna, her eyes wide. "Can we have one this year, please, Jimmy?"

The strain in James' eyes grew more evident. He ran a hand through his sister's grubby hair. "We'll have to see what Father Christmas brings."

Donna's grin widened. "Father Christmas brought me a whole orange to school last year."

"I remember." James chuckled, then turned to Edith.

"Really, thank you," he said softly. "She's always so happy after a day of school. I'm really grateful to you and your mother."

"It's our pleasure," said Edith. "She's so sweet and cheerful." She paused, scraping for something to say, not wanting James to go so soon.

"We'll decorate the school the week before Christmas. The children are very excited."

"Oh, I know." James laughed. "It's all she ever talks about. And best of all, last Sunday when we were on our way to the chapel, she read a sign for some Christmas special offers to me out loud." His eyes were shining. "She can read."

Edith knew that, at the age of fourteen, James was still completely illiterate. "She's a very clever girl," she said.

Donna basked under the compliment, clinging tightly to James.

"Well, I think she has two very good teachers, too," said James softly. He patted Donna's head.

"Come on now, pet. Time to go home."

"Have you eaten anything yet today, James?" asked Mama suddenly. Edith hadn't realized that her mother was standing right behind her.

James hesitated for a beat too long. "Yes, ma'am," he said, touching his grubby cap.

"Well, it won't hurt to have something for the road, in any case," said Mama briskly. She held out a tiny parcel wrapped in brown paper.

Edith knew it contained the heel of bread that they were going to have with their soup that night. "Here you are."

"Ma'am, I couldn't…" James began.

"Yes, you could, and you're going to." Mama thrust it into his hands. "Take care of yourself now, my boy. Go on then. Get home before it gets too late."

Still protesting faintly, James shuffled off, bending down to lift Donna onto his hip as they exited the courtyard. The little girl's head slumped onto his shoulder, and Edith guessed that she was fast asleep by the time his tall figure faded into the darkening streets.

Edith was missing that heel of bread when she got into bed that evening. Their supper had been a watery soup made with fish chunks and turnips, and while it was good to have something warm in her stomach, she wasn't quite full.

Still, an extra cup of tea almost made up for it, and Edith knew that she wasn't too hungry to fall asleep. Those nights were the worst nights. At least this wouldn't be one of them.

The fire burned low in the room's small hearth as Edith pulled the covers up to her chin, flexing her feet inside the woolly socks Mama had knitted for her the year before. They were a bit threadbare now, but they still did their job. Mama was already in bed, reading by firelight, her eyes squinting down at the page. She had to hold the spine of the book very carefully; it was starting to come to pieces.

"What are you reading?" Edith asked, cuddling a little closer to Mama.

Mama put her free arm around Edith's shoulders. "*Moby-Dick*."

"That's a special favourite of yours."

"Yes, it is." Mama chuckled softly. "I was reading it when I met your father, you know."

Edith held her breath. Since Papa had died four years ago, Mama hardly ever spoke of him. She waited eagerly to hear a little more. She'd only been eight when Papa died, and though her memories of him were vivid, she wished she had more of them.

"I was sitting on a wall in the countryside where we both lived then," said Mama softly. "I was meant to be going into town with my sisters, but oh – they were just so frivolous, and I knew that my papa wanted me to marry that dreadful Richard Hattington, and I couldn't face it. So I was hiding in the fields and reading *Moby-Dick*; it had just come out that year. Your papa told me that I made a funny face while I was reading. We fell in love right away." Mama sighed with pleasure. "It took Papa a little while to agree to our marriage, of course. And then we came here to open your papa's carpentry shop."

Edith knew the rest of the story; that Papa had died from consumption four years ago, and Mama had been forced to sell the shop, but managed to keep the house and open the dame school.

She loved the dame school, but she missed the days when she and Mama would play all day, and then Papa would come home and throw her high into the air with his booming laugh.

"I miss him," she said softly.

Mama kissed her cheek. "I know, my pet," she said.

"But we're getting by all right without him. We've got each other, and something to eat, and a few little treats at Christmastime, and we can help the hungry; and that's more than a lot of folk have."

The hungry. Edith thought of James. "I'm worried about James," she said, adding hastily, "and Donna."

"I know." Mama sighed.

"There are bruises on Donna's arms today." Edith bit her lip. "I know James didn't do that to her."

"Of course not. That boy would rather die than hurt his sister, and I mean that literally," said Mama firmly. "It's that father of theirs, drunken layabout that he is."

"At least he sends Donna to school."

"James sends Donna to school. I don't think their father knows that Donna isn't already working – he would force her to work, if he knew."

Mama ran a hand through Edith's hair. "But don't worry about it too much, my dear. You're doing all you can for them. And James is doing the right thing for Donna."

Mama kissed Edith's hair.

"With an education, you can improve your station in life so much. That's my hope for you, too. One day, with your education, you're going to leave all this behind. You'll never be hungry again, or cold. You'll have a nice house and a good husband, and a tree and a goose every Christmas."

"And you," said Edith quickly.

"And me." Mama chuckled softly, closing her book. "Now let's go to sleep, poppet. Dream of Christmas, and all the joy it brings."

Edith laid her head down on her mother's shoulder, cuddled close against her, and closed her eyes. The thought of never being hungry again was a nice one, but all the same, Edith felt she had everything she truly needed right here beside her.

Chapter Two

There was a hollow, echoing quality to the wind that shrieked and bellowed around the eaves of the house, rattling its windows like some angry monster trying to find its way in.

Swirls of snow were hurled down the street, heaping up in frigid piles against the walls. The children sat wrapped in tattered rugs in front of the coal stove, drinking hot tea while Mama read to them. All the children, that was, except one.

Edith pressed herself against the kitchen counter, peering through the cracked windowpane into the street. The first week of December had arrived with a vengeance. Her nose burned with cold, even though she was wrapped in both the coats that she owned.

When her breath fogged on the glass, it only made it seem colder outside. She used her sleeve to clean off the glass with a squeaking noise.

"Come away from the window, dear," said Mama, pausing in her reading. "You'll catch your death standing in that draft."

"Where are they?" Edith asked, worry and frustration boiling up in her voice.

"They'll be here. Don't worry," said Mama. "Now come away there."

Edith stepped back reluctantly, and just then, she caught a glimpse of two figures coming down the street: one tall and thin, one short and squat. Hurrying to the door, she flung it open as they approached through the swirling snow.

Donna looked squat today because she was wrapped in a coat so much too big for her that it dragged behind her like an emperor's train. Snowflakes had gathered on it, and when the little girl reached the front door, Edith saw that the hem of the coat was frosted.

"Good morning, Donna!" she gushed, relief flooding her body. Donna gave her a haunted look, then shuffled past her into the house.

"Donna!" said Edith, shocked by the little girl's rudeness. She turned to judge James' reaction, but he was already hurrying across the courtyard and back into the street.

"James!" Edith took a few steps towards him, snowflakes swirling against her face with breath-taking cold.

He turned. "I'm sorry, Edith," he said. "I'm late to work. I have to go."

He was in his shirtsleeves; the tip of his nose was blue with cold, and though his hands were buried in his pockets and his tall frame crumpled up in an effort to conserve warmth.

Edith could see him shivering. The wind whipped at his much-patched blue shirt, making it snap against his bony body.

"James, where's your coat?" Edith asked.

"I have to go," he repeated, turning, and this time she saw it: an ugly, dark purple stain across his face — a fresh bruise obscuring most of his left cheek.

"James, what happened?" Donna cried.

But her words were torn away by the wind. James had already hurried out into the snow

∼ ∼ ∼ ∼ ∼

The morning was desperately busy. It was now less than three weeks to Christmas, and the children were excited and chaotic through morning lessons as Mama read to them from the Gospel of Luke and had them rehearse parts of *A Christmas Carol* to re-enact for their parents in a few weeks' time.

It was only much later in the morning that Edith was finally able to find a moment to talk to Mama. The children were sitting quietly in the classroom, tired from the morning's excitement, making paper chains with bits of old newspaper for decorations.

Where Edith stood at the kitchen table, she could look through the door and into the classroom. Donna was sitting alone in a corner, making her chains slowly, her eyes red-rimmed and unfocused.

Edith cut another thin slice of rough bread, her heart aching with worry. Mama came in a few seconds later, carrying a bucket of water from the pump at the end of the street.

"Mama, I think something's wrong," said Edith.

Mama set the bucket down with a huff of effort, then straightened slowly, stretching out her back. "With Donna?" she said.

"Yes. And not just Donna." Edith set down the bread knife, turning to face Mama. "James, too."

"I didn't see him this morning."

"I did. He wasn't wearing a coat... he'd given it to Donna. He seemed so cold." Edith shivered. "And he had a bruise on his face, too. An ugly one." She said it almost hesitantly, knowing that Mama would be upset.

She was right. Mama shook her head, pressing her mouth into a thin line of bitterness. "That father of theirs!" she muttered angrily, slamming the kettle down onto the floor with unnecessary force. "I worry about Donna. She's very quiet today; nothing like her usual self. I thought perhaps she was sick."

"I'm worried about James, out there in this weather without a coat," said Edith. "I hope the costermonger helps him."

"He's a good man. He probably will," said Mama. She lifted the bucket with a grunt, pouring water into the kettle. "But I'll speak to James when he gets back."

"Isn't there something we can do?" Edith asked. "Oh, Mama, their papa hurts them. I know he does. We can't just let that keep on happening without doing a thing to help them."

Tears burned at the back of her eyes, making them sting. "He's the one who hit James, I know it, and he hurts Donna, too. Please, Mama, please, we have to do something."

"Dearest Edie!" Mama put the kettle down on the coal stove and turned to Edith, wrapping her in a hug. She held her very tightly for a few long moments, then murmured into Edith's red hair. "Never change, my love."

"What do you mean?" Edith asked, confused.

Mama stepped back, holding Edith's hands. "I don't want you to ever stop caring about what happens to others," she said. "There's a good deal too much selfishness in this city, and we must never become that way. We must always believe in helping one another; it's the only way we can leave this world a little better than when we arrived in it." She squeezed Edith's hands. "You love Christmas so much. This is deep at the heart of Christmas and its magic: caring for others, even if it means disadvantaging ourselves."

Edith sniffed, tears still threatening to spill over. "Donna can't come to school at Christmas," she said. "She and James will be stuck at home with their father, and there's... there's no telling what he will do." Fear gripped her. "Mama, please, is there nothing we can do?"

"There are things we can do, my pet." Mama kissed Edith's forehead. "We can try to help them. But it might mean that we have to give some things up."

"What kinds of things?" asked Edith.

"The little treats we like so much at Christmas." Mama put her head to one side, studying Edith's face. "We might not be able to have oranges and presents and a tree this year, my darling, if we help James and Donna as you said."

Edith bit her lip. She did love the little things that made Christmas so special, but the thought of leaving Donna and James to have a cold, hungry, frightening Christmas at home with their father was much worse. She wasn't sure what Mama was planning, but she trusted her with it.

"It's all right, Mama," she said. "There are more important things than that. And didn't you say that Christmas magic wasn't about presents?"

Pride shone in Mama's eyes, making tears pool within them. "That's my girl," she whispered, giving Edith another warm hug. "Now try not to worry too much. Help me get their lunch ready, there's a good girl. Leave James and his sister to me."

Relief lifted Edith's shoulders as she turned back to cutting the thin slices of bread. Each child would receive only one with a cup of weak tea, but that wasn't what had been worrying Edith so deeply today. Instead, she felt as though she could breathe easy again.

She knew that once Mama made up her mind to help someone, nothing would stop her.

~ ~ ~ ~ ~

As usual, Donna was the last child to go home that evening. She lay sleeping on a rug in front of the stove, clutching her little doll.

There had been no playing today, but she hadn't let the doll out of her sight, keeping a firm grip on it. Her body was wrapped around it now, her hair draping over her shoulders, as limp and tired as the look on her sleeping face.

Edith sat at the kitchen table, keeping half an eye on Donna as she tried to read. Mama was planning lessons for the next day. James was even later than usual. The wind howled outside, a haunted sound echoing around the house, and Edith clutched the book tightly, unable to focus on a single word. The thought of him out there in the cold was unthinkable.

Finally, his usual knock came at the door, and Edith leaped to her feet as though her chair was spring-loaded. She rushed to the door, flinging it wide. James stood on the threshold, his hair in disarray, his eyes red and tired.

The bruise on his face had deepened to blacks and purples that looked too mangled to be real human skin. He blinked at her for a few long moments, utter exhaustion in his eyes.

Edith saw that he was wearing a makeshift coat: an old hessian sack with holes cut for his head and arms.

It made him look even more like a scarecrow with the tattered ends of the sack trailing down around his knees.

"James!" said Edith. "I've been so worried. Are you all right? What happened to your face? Come inside for tea – I've made some – it's nice and warm – "

James held up a hand, stopping her in her tracks. "Thank you," he said softly, "but I won't be long. Is Donna here?"

"She's asleep," said Edith, "but..."

"Good." James sighed, running a hand through his hair. He wouldn't meet her eyes. "I need to talk to your mama, please."

Edith turned, but Mama was already walking into the kitchen, her arms wrapped around her body against the icy draft coming through the door. "James, dear, come inside," she said.

"I can't, ma'am," James began.

Mama reached out, grabbed his arm, pulled him into the kitchen, and closed the door gently behind him.

"Sit," she said. "It's time we had a little chat."

James sank into a chair, staring at Mama with wide eyes. Mama poured him a tin mug of weak tea and placed it in front of him. "You're dreadfully cold. Drink that," she commanded.

No one dared contradict Mama if she was in a mood like this. Edith sat down next to her, pride and love bubbling up inside her as Mama took her place opposite James and fixed him with her most serious expression.

Nothing could stop Mama, Edith knew it, and because of Mama, it made it a little easier to see James like this: with his eyes so red, and goosebumps on his bare neck, and the way his hands trembled as he clutched the tea and sipped it with a pathetic attempt to hide his desperation.

It was only after half the tea was gone that James spoke.

"Mrs. Atkinson, I... I have some bad news."

A hunted look came into his eyes.

"I have to take Donna out of your school. My father…" Pain flashed across his face. "We can't stay with him anymore. He hurts Donna. I want her to have an education more than anything, but the way he treats her… I'm so afraid he'll… he'll kill her."

Tears glittered briefly in his eyes, and he dashed them away. "Hopefully it will only be for a little while. I want to bring her back, I truly do. But for now we have to find somewhere to live… and the rent… Donna will have to go to work. A friend of mine has found a place for her… in the match factory."

Edith's heart squeezed. She had seen the match girls pass by their house sometimes on their way home from work, very late in the night; pale, thin creatures, their eyes hollow, many of them with bloodstained scarves wrapped around their faces to hide the rotting flesh of their cancerous jaws.

The thought of Donna in such a place made her shattered. She leaned forward. "Mama – "

Mama reached over the table, laying a hand over James'. "You don't have to do that, James."

"Please, Mrs. Atkinson, I have no other choice." James blinked at his tears again. "We have nowhere else to go."

"Yes, you do." Mama smiled. "You can stay here."

"Here?" James' eyes widened, and hope sparkled in them briefly until it was crushed by sheer force of habit.

Edith had never seen him desolate like this before, but then again, she had seldom ever seen him without Donna before.

She knew she had underestimated the pain and worry in him; he hid it well, for Donna's sake. "Ma'am, I don't have the money," he whispered. "I can't..."

"Don't worry about the money," said Mama. "You don't have to pay for Donna's schooling. She can help us in the house when the other children have gone home, and whatever you earn at the costermonger's can be used to help with your keep."

"Of course, ma'am, of course, all of it," said James eagerly. "But please – I know you're not well off – and – "

"It's nearly Christmas, darling," said Mama, softening. "We are better off giving at this time of the year. Come. Let me help you. It will be good, in any case, to have a young man around who can help us to mend the things that need mending; and Edith spends hardly any time with children her own age as it is."

"Mrs. Atkinson..." James made no effort to blink away the tears this time.

Mama got to her feet, brushing off her skirt in a business-like way. "It's almost time for supper. Edith, get some spare rugs for James and Donna, and he can make up a bed for them on the kitchen floor in front of the stove. Donna and I will get supper ready."

"Mrs. Atkinson," said James again.

Mama raised an eyebrow at him. "I think I told you to get started on making your bed, young man."

"Yes, ma'am," said James, then cleared his throat. "Thank you."

Mama smiled just a little then, and in her warm eyes, Edith saw something she hadn't expected: utter contentment.

As if Mama was the one who had just received some rare and precious gift. "None of that, now," she said. "Get to work."

"Yes, ma'am," said James again.

Edith grabbed Mama's hand as James got up and turned away. "Thank you, Mama," she breathed.

Mama kissed the top of her head, softening a little. "Try not to forget this, my darling," she said, tracing a finger along Edith's cheek. "Never forget this Christmas."

Mama had no idea, at the time, how impossible it would become for Edith to ever wipe this Christmas from her memory.

Chapter Three

Edith could hear James' voice booming through the courtyard as he approached the back door. It had only recently broken, and there was still a husky quality to it that she liked. She smiled to herself as she straightened the little holly wreath in the middle of the kitchen table.

There were no ribbons on the wreath this year, and they had gathered the holly themselves from the park; she supposed that she did miss the ribbons a little, but the bright red berries almost made up for their absence. She seized a dishcloth from behind the door and knelt to open the stove and check on the baking bread.

Outside, as James drew nearer, the words of his carolling became audible. "… the blazing Yule before us, fa-la-la-la-la, la-la-la-la," he was singing. "Strike the harp and join the chorus."

Edith joined in as the door swung open and he stepped into the kitchen, snowflakes glittering on his shoulders and the too-big cap that Mama had scrounged for him from somewhere.

"Follow me in merry measure, while I tell of Yuletide treasure," they chorused. "Fa-la-la-la-la, la-la-la-la!"

Edith's voice broke a little on the last note, and she giggled as she set the fresh bread down on the top of the stove, clapping an embarrassed hand to her throat.

"It's a Christmas carol, Edith," said James, his eyes dancing. "Not a Christmas croak."

"You're a fine one to talk!" Edith flicked at him playfully with the dishcloth.

It had only been a few weeks now since James and Donna had come to stay with Mama and Edith, but already, James looked fuller, stronger.

Perhaps no less scarecrow-like; after all, there had not been very much to go around even before he and Donna had come.

But there was colour in his cheeks now, and light in his eyes, even when Donna wasn't around.

"Well, don't stop now," said Mama's cheerful voice. She came bustling into the kitchen, Donna tagging close behind her. "There's still time for another carol while we butter the bread. There's still a little butter, isn't there, Edith?"

"There is, Mama," said Edith, who had been saving it all week for this morning.

"Good!" said Mama. "And we can take that last jar of strawberry jam from the pantry; it is Christmas morning, after all. With a bit of tea, and half an orange each, I think that will do us quite nicely."

Edith's heart faltered a little within her at the realization that today would be a hungry day again, until supper, at least.

And even then, there would be no roast chicken and potatoes; Mama had told her quietly last night that they could have some fresh fish, and maybe make some chips, but there would be no sweet treats.

For the first time since Edith could remember, she had woken this morning with no little brown parcel at the foot of her bed.

Mama's parcels were always little things – maybe an orange and some chestnuts to roast over the fire, or a little dress made of rags for her doll when Edith had been younger – but the absence of one had stung more than Edith had expected.

"It sounds very nice, ma'am," said James, and he meant it. Edith wondered if he had ever had anything nice for Christmas at all, and her dismay melted like frost in sunlight.

She found her smile returning. "All right, then," she said. "Let's cut the bread – and how about 'Away in a Manger'?"

"No, no!" said Donna, her eyes lighting up. "There's a pretty one about ships – we sang it last year at our Christmas play."

"Very well, then," said Mama, laughing. She started singing in her fine, bell-like voice. "I saw three ships come sailing in on Christmas Day, on Christmas Day…"

Edith's eyes met James'. There was joy in them, but something more, too: relief, and utter gratitude. Perhaps that could be gift enough for her this year.

She added her voice to the chorus, and felt more than heard James joining in. "I saw three ships come sailing in on Christmas Day in the morning!"

~ ~ ~ ~ ~

Mama held her arms up over her head, hands flopping over, and gave Donna an expectant look. The little girl's eyes narrowed in contemplation. "Rabbit?" she guessed.

Mama shook her head.

"Um... unicorn?" Donna's eyes widened with excitement.

Visibly more frustrated, Mama shook her head again and started walking around with exaggerated, shuffling steps. Edith stifled a giggle.

"I don't know," said Donna, flapping her hands and bouncing in her seat. "Cow? Bull? Is it a – "

"Time's up!" said James triumphantly, gesturing at the clock with the cracked face against the wall.

Mama dropped her arms to her sides. "Donkey!" she said, laughing.

"You can't call me a donkey!" said Donna.

"No, you silly thing!" Mama swept Donna into her arms and took her place on the threadbare sofa, cuddling the little girl close. "The charade was a donkey."

"Oh." Donna laughed. "Those were ears!"

"They *were* ears." Mama smiled over at Edith. "I think Edith knew the moment she saw me."

"That's exactly why you two are not allowed to be in a team together. You're just too good at it," said James. "It's like you can read one another's minds."

Edith wasn't so sure about reading minds during charades, but she was reading Mama's mind right now as she looked into her laughing eyes. She had seldom ever seen her mother this happy. Not since Papa had died, anyway.

Even though her belly was already stinging with hunger, and Christmas supper was still hours away, Edith almost wanted to stop time right here. Seeing Mama like this made Edith happier than she could ever remember being. And maybe having James by her side like this had something to do with it, too.

"Is it our turn now?" asked James.

"Actually, I think we've come to a draw," said Mama. "I think we should go." She got up, setting Donna down on the floor.

"Go?" asked Edith. "Where?" She glanced at the clock again; it was one o' clock in the afternoon, and every Christmas that she could remember, Mama had taken her out to the bakery at this time on Christmas Day to choose one sweet treat.

It could only be one, but she could choose anything she liked. Last year, she had agonized over choosing between a fat mince pie and one of those white shepherd's crook-shaped sugar sticks that she loved.

Yesterday, though, Mama had told her that they couldn't afford it this Christmas.

"Well, I think it would be lovely to take a little walk in the streets and look at the beautiful Christmas lights and decorations everyone has put up," said Mama. "What do you think, Edie?"

"I love the lights," said Donna. "I want to see them. Please."

"I love the lights, too." Edith grinned at her, taking her hand. "Let's go!"

A few minutes later, they were all walking down the street together, heading to the same little market square where the bakery was. Even though Edith's mouth watered with longing thoughts of candies and mints and toffees, she still felt a bubble of excitement in her belly as she held Mama's hand. It was hard not to.

Even here in the streets near home, an effort had been made to decorate for Christmas. Ramshackle houses with gaps in the roofs and cracks in the walls still somehow had candles in the window.

One home's walls leaned on one another like a group of wounded soldiers, yet a browned and wilting wreath, crumpled as though it had been picked out of the rubbish somewhere, still hung on the flaking front door.

As they grew nearer to the nicer part of town where the square was, there were more and more decorations to be seen.

Bright holly and mistletoe and bunting hung between the eaves of the shops and houses; there were candles and gas lights everywhere, shining brightly in the muted afternoon light.

The sky was pale grey, but the soft snowflakes that tumbled and twirled in the still air made up for the lack of sunlight, sparkling where they settled on Mama's hair and eyelashes.

Donna was skipping next to James ahead of Mama and Edith, the gap in the bottom of her left shoe flashing with every step, but right now she had forgotten her own poverty in favour of the beauty surrounding her.

The streets were busy, too. People strode hither and thither, carrying brown paper parcels in their arms, bright with ribbons. There was none of the muffled hurry of a weekday afternoon, however. Everyone was strolling, laughing on their way to some party or another; it was as though the whole city had slowed down just a little. Some people even called out "Merry Christmas!" as they passed, even though they were perfect strangers.

There was a clatter of hooves and a jingle of harness bells, and a splendid four-in-hand strode down the street towards them, the handsome hackneys throwing their polished hooves high with every stride, their manes streaming with ribbons and harness bright with silver bells.

It rushed right past Mama and the others, plumes dancing high on the horses' heads.

"Keep a good hand on her there, James," said Mama.

"I've got her, ma'am," said James, gripping Donna's hand a little more tightly.

A group of carollers came past them: ladies and gentlemen all in long white robes, carrying golden candles in their hands that lit up the grey day.

The sound of their united voices rose and fell in the air, entwining with the snowflakes, so beautiful it was nearly palpable, like a silver thread uniting the beauty of the afternoon with everyone inside it. "O holy night! The stars are brightly shining, it is the night of our dear Saviour's birth. Long lay the world in sin and error pining till He appeared and the Spirit felt its worth."

When they turned into the market square, Edith couldn't help but gasp with awe. A full-size Christmas tree had been set up in the middle of the square. It towered over them, all ribbons and bunting and white canes hanging from its branches; there were oranges on it too, and brightly wrapped toffees, and a glittering silver star on the very top.

"Oh! Oh!" gasped Donna. "Look at it! Just look at it!" She tugged at James' hand.

"Slowly, Donnie." James laughed. "We'll go and have a closer look in a second."

Donna was bouncing up and down, towing James from one window to the other as she excitedly pointed out the decorations in all the windows. The shops were all closed and sleepy, of course, except for the little bakery that capitalized on Christmas shoppers looking for something fresh; but the decorations were still out in them, and Donna's face was transfixed with joy.

James pretended to be looking at the decorations, but Edith could see that he was really looking at Donna, and his eyes were shining.

She gave Mama's hand a little squeeze. "I wonder if they've ever done this before," she said. "Been able to see some Christmas magic, instead of just having to worry about their father all day."

Mama smiled at Edith. "Your heart is beautiful, my dear," she said. "Never lose your faith in that, or in the beauty that Christmas brings."

The streets were busier here.

The jingle of bells and merry clopping of hooves filled the air as carriages trotted to and fro. A young lady in fine clothes was bustling down the street towards them, so laden with parcels that she could barely see.

There was a wide smile behind the parcels, though, and she seemed to be hurrying excitedly to some gathering or another. Disaster struck when she was a few feet away from James and her foot caught on an uneven cobblestone.

She tripped, just managing to stay on her feet; but the parcels cascaded to the ground. One of them burst, and marbles rolled everywhere, sparkling.

"Oh! Are you all right?" asked James, towing Donna over to where the young lady was frantically trying to pick everything up again.

"Quite all right, young man." She laughed, embarrassed. "Just clumsy."

"Here – let me help you." James bent down to pick up some of the marbles.

"Thank you! My nephew does love marbles, but they're not very easy to wrap." The young lady laughed, scooping some of them back into the paper.

"Donnie, dear, stand very still now," said James, letting go of his sister's hand. "Let me help the young lady quickly."

"All right," said Donna obediently.

"I should take her hand," said Edith, quickening her stride.

She was still a few yards away from Donna when it happened. A gust of wind sent a swirl of snowflakes across the market square, sparkling in the candlelight.

The wind caught at one of the bright red ribbons on the Christmas tree, pulling it loose and sending it floating across the square.

Donna, who had been staring at the tree in rapture, gave a cry of delight as it floated towards her. It was as though the wind itself was bringing the gift to her little hands.

The gust fell a little short, however. It blew itself out, and the ribbon landed softly in the street, just a few feet away from Donna. The little girl was transfixed. She rushed forward with a cry of joy, her hands extended towards the ribbon, just as the carriage came galloping around the corner.

It was filled with young, whooping men, their voices too loud and filled with drunken glee; the horse was in a white-whipped lather, its driver lashing its haunches and jerking at the reins, its head so high that it couldn't see what was in front of it, especially not the little girl that ran forward right under its flashing hooves.

Edith started forward, but Mama had already passed her, already flung a hand back into Edith's shoulder with enough force that she fell to the ground.

When she rolled onto her side, it was all happening right in front of her and she could do nothing to stop it. Donna looking up at the speeding horse heading for her.

The piercing whistle of the child's scream cut off short. Mama flinging herself into the street, her outstretched hands slamming into Donna's side, throwing her out of the way.

The thump as Mama landed heavily on the street. The screams from the passers-by.

The crunch of hooves. The blood on the cobblestones.

Edith screamed, lunging to her feet: the scene before her was a blur of cartwheels, of people tumbling everywhere, of blood, the shattering of carriage wood, the flash of horseshoes as everything fell over and around everything else. Beyond it all, an unknown gentleman clutching an unhurt Donna in his arms.

And in the midst of the carnage, Mama. A crumpled form, pale, bleeding, motionless.

Edith rushed forward, still screaming till it felt that her throat was bleeding, but before she could reach the end of the pavement, a strong arm was flung around her chest. James seized her, turning her so that her face was pressed against him, wrapping his arms around her, strong as chains.

"Let me go! Let me go! Mama! Mama!" Edith shrieked.

"Don't look. Don't look, Edie." James held her tighter, too tight to escape. "Don't look up. You don't need to see it."

Edith screamed and fought against him, but he was too strong. "Mama!" she screamed. "Mama!"

James held her more tightly, his body trembling violently.

His hand held the back of her head pressing her face into his shoulder. "There's nothing you can do," he said.

The realization, the honesty and grief in his voice, sapped the strength from her body all in a rush. It felt as though her joints had turned into ice water. She collapsed against him, sick to her stomach, her world spinning, clinging to James with all the strength she had.

His voice was as heavy as a tombstone.

"There's nothing anyone can do."

Chapter Four

It was New Year's Day, but nothing about it felt like a fresh beginning. To Edith, it was the end of her world.

There was no snow today. Just a slate-grey sky, low and heavy as Edith's heart, and a restless, anxious wind that plucked at the skirt of the black dress that Timmy's mother had cobbled together for her from when she had mourned Timmy's younger sister.

She kept her eyes on the hem of that dress, unable to look up, staring instead at her worn and cracked shoes as they took one step after the other along the cobbled street to the tiny local church.

Just a week ago, she had walked this very street with Mama's warm, living hand in her own. She had been so happy. She tried to recall the feeling now, but it was met with a terrible pang of agony that sent fresh tears cascading down her cheeks.

It was as though grief had robbed her not only of her present happiness, but also of all the joy she could ever remember; every happy memory she had was now too painful to recall, and the inside of her heart felt red and raw, as though a hot poker had been brutally thrust through it.

She only glanced up a little from time to time to make sure she was not too close behind the pallbearers.

There were four of them, papas of the children who attended Mama's dame school – of the children who used to attend Mama's dame school.

Their Sunday best was as ragged and badly fitting as the dress Edith now wore, but there was no price to be placed on how straight their backs were, or how smartly they marched with the coffin on their shoulders.

Mama's coffin.

It was too heavy a thought to be contained in Edith's body. She lowered her eyes again, feeling more adrift and lost than anything else. Like she was separated from the world by a wall of glass; she knew what she should be feeling, knew in some part of her what was happening, but could not comprehend it.

Her tears were more confusion than pain. She wanted to ask Mama how to deal with this; wanted to tell her everything she was feeling now. But every time she looked around for her mother, she wasn't there. It was like stumbling in the same pothole over and over and over again.

The minister had to stop talking twice, his voice too thickened by tears, when he gave the last sermon for which some part of Mama would ever be present at the graveside.

The earth looked so cold. Edith tried not to stare at it or at how small the coffin looked in there. It was so puny, considering it contained her entire world. She tried not to listen to the sniffles around her. Many people had come.

Everyone loved Mama. Everyone *had* loved Mama. Mama had taught Edith her tenses so well. Why had they suddenly become so difficult now?

She was the first to start filling the grave.

She knew everyone was looking at her when she dug her fingers into the cold, cold soil and hesitated for a long moment, staring down at the wooden surface of the coffin.

She should feel something, she knew. Like she was burying her mother. But it didn't feel like her mother was in there. It didn't feel like Mama was here at all, and that was worse somehow.

She dropped the soil onto the lid of the coffin. And the hollow *thunk* it made echoed into every corner of her world.

~ ~ ~ ~ ~

For all that the people had been staring at her while she cast the first handful of soil into Mama's grave, and for all that they had come together to help with the funeral, it was as though all their grief ended with that ceremony.

Someone had brought them some soup for supper that night, and she'd heard people at the funeral muttering behind their hands about what would happen to those poor children.

One of them had been Mr. Wilkes, the patriarch who lived at the top of the street. He was something of an unofficial leader of the little community; too rich to need the dame school, but not rich enough to be oblivious to its existence.

Edith had been sitting at the foot of Mama's grave, just staring at it, while people milled around after the service was finished. She had heard Mr. Wilkes' voice booming through the crowd and glanced over listlessly to see him in a huddle with one or two older women and the minister.

"It's a tragedy, reverend," Mr. Wilkes had said pompously. "A terrible disservice to our entire street, so it is. It's only a mercy she had had the foresight to put money aside for the burial."

"Mrs. Atkinson was very loved." The minister had dried his eyes. "And that poor child. Just four years ago, I was standing in this very graveyard, officiating her father's ceremony."

"Yes, pity be, she's an orphan now." one of the older women had gasped.

Orphan. The word had struck Edith with a leaden thump, like something dead and disgusting landing over her shoulders.

"Yes," said the minister.

"What about those other two youngsters?" asked Mr. Wilkes.

"James and Donna? They're as good as orphaned too. Their mother long gone, and their father such a drunkard as to hardly ever be coherent."

"Then what will become of them?" the woman had asked.

A silence had fallen.

"Surely, Susan Atkinson's daughter can't go into the..." Mr. Wilkes hadn't said the word that Edith knew he was thinking: *workhouse*. The very implication had sent a terrible chill through her body, the first real emotion she had felt in days. She hardly knew who she was anymore, but she did know this: the workhouse was a place she would never, ever go. Mama had always said so.

"No," said the minister firmly. "None of that. That young James makes some money. He told me that he will find work for the girls, too."

"But where will they live?"

"In Susan's house. Legally, Susan left everything to Edith."

"Edith will need a ward, then," said Mr. Wilkes.

"None of us can care for her." The minister's voice had been leaden with sorrow and truth. "But we can make sure that no one ever finds her to take her and the other two out of that house. Susan was a bright light in our community. Surely, this is one last thing we can do for her, even if we cannot care for Edith the way she would have wanted."

His voice had been filled with guilt, and Edith had felt some vague flicker of relief. Perhaps she had even hoped that the community would go beyond merely turning a blind eye to their presence in Mama's house.

But the next day, when Edith woke alone in the vastness of the double bed, there was no one. Everyone had gone on with their lives, fulfilled by the funeral, feeling like they'd done Mama one last service

She sat on the front step of the house that no longer felt like home somehow, staring down the empty street, barely noticing the icy breeze that prickled her skin through the threadbare fabric of her dress.

There were no more Christmas decorations anymore, except for a few leaves of mistletoe, wilted and trampled in the gutter. Even the pretty snowflakes were gone; instead, the world was covered in a greying, yellowed slush that smelled like cat urine. People were hurrying up and down the street. Some of them had hugged her at the funeral.

No one looked at her now, just a crumpled little figure in a mourning dress that was much too big, staring into a world that suddenly contained no more joy.

She didn't realize that she was cold until a rug settled over her, gentle hands tucking it around her shoulders. The warmth of someone sat down beside her, and a tin mug was held out to her, containing weak, yellow tea. "You looked cold," said James.

She took the tea automatically, clinging to the tiny scrap of pleasure she felt at the warmth of the mug in her hands. "Thank you."

James stared down at nothing. He didn't ask how she was; he didn't need to.

"Edith," he began, instead. "I... I should never have let go of Donna's hand."

Edith looked up at him, surprised by the raw pain in his voice. "What?"

He raised his face. His eyes were glimmering with tears. "It's my fault," he whispered. "I shouldn't have let her go. If I hadn't let her go..."

Edith supposed she should feel a pang of anger. But looking into his anguished eyes, it was impossible. She remembered the force with which Mama had pushed her aside, the determination in Mama's eyes as she lived her last moments, the inevitability of it all.

"It wasn't your fault," said Edith. She found the strength to reach over and put a hand awkwardly on his arm. "It wasn't anyone's fault. It was just an accident, James. I know you love Mama, and so does Donna..." She pressed the heels of her hands into her eyes. "Why did she have to die? It's all so... so... so empty. It's like nothing matters. Nothing in this world matters."

She began to sob, great chunks of grief ripping loose from inside her chest and spilling out through her eyes. James wrapped an arm around her and held her tightly under his arm, and she cried and cried. She had not only lost Mama; it was though all the magic in the whole world had disappeared.

Everything she believed in, everything Mama had believed in, lay in tatters around her feet. Mama had believed in love and hope and kindness and magic, but it had all been crushed in one terrible instant.

"I'm here. I'm here," said James. "I'm here for you, Edie." He patted her back. "Now come on. Take a sip of your tea. You'll feel just a little better."

Edith shakily obeyed, swallowing the tea along with some of her tears. She wiped at her eyes and grimaced. She'd never tasted tea quite so weak before.

James gave a long, slow sigh, like he was letting out all his worry gently to avoid scaring her. "That was… our last bit of tea," he said slowly.

Edith looked up at him. She realized that she should be afraid, should be thinking of what to do. She knew she couldn't run the dame school on her own. No one would send children to her, a twelve-year-old girl.

"I can't open the dame school again," she said.

"No… no. And we don't need more attention on us in this house than necessary, even though Mr. Wilkes and the minister agreed not to tell anyone that we're living here."

James paused, struggling manfully with his emotions for a moment, then took a deep breath. "But it's going to be all right. I spoke to the costermonger. He has work for all three of us, if you and Donna can sell flowers, and I can go on with our work, we can stay in the house, I think. Your mama had no family, and no one will come to claim it, I don't think. It's too small. So we'll just stay here and work and be together, and everything will be all right." He squeezed her shoulders. "Everything will be all right

Edith wanted to be worried, or grateful, or anything. But all of this simply fell into the black hole of her grief. So she just nodded, and thanked him, but she didn't believe him.

Nothing could ever be all right again.

Chapter Five

"Mignonettes." Edith tried to raise her voice above a sad croak, but it was difficult given the weight of the tears that seemed ready to strangle her. "Pretty sprigs of mignonettes. Get your mignonettes!"

She managed a little volume on the last word, but it became a desperate squawk instead, and the gentleman hurrying past her on the street gave her an uncomfortable glance before tugging his coat collar a little bit higher and rushing off into the crowd.

Edith flinched, glancing over her shoulder at where Mr. Thompson was standing by the handcart. He never struck the palms of her hands.

He didn't want them disfigured where they clutched at the sad little sprigs of bright white flowers, which wilted now, drooping sadly over her fingers. Instead, it was her calves that burned. He kept a special cane in his cart just for the purpose of hitting one of the children when they misbehaved.

This time, though, Mr. Thompson hadn't been looking. He was busy helping James to pack his oranges, carrots, beets and turnips back into the cart; it must be almost time to head home.

Edith felt relief, or at least, she knew that it was appropriate to feel relief right now. It had been a long time since her heart had felt anything, except that it was falling and falling through a bottomless pit, helpless in the utter dark.

"Violets, cut violets," piped a tiny, hollow voice beside her. "A violet for your lady, sir?" Donna stepped out into the street, pathetically holding up a little bunch of the flowers tied off with a bit of grubby string.

An old gentleman who had been hurrying past paused to looked down at her, something softening in his eyes as he gazed at the flowers. "Ah, violets," he murmured. "My wife's favourite flowers."

"Perhaps she would like some, sir," quavered Donna.

The gentleman's eyes narrowed suddenly. "My wife's been dead five years," he spat. "Get away from me, you stupid little child."

Donna's face froze as though she'd been slapped, and Edith felt a strange, boiling sensation in the pit of her stomach. It took her a second to recognize the emotion as anger, and it felt so good to feel something – anything – that she leaned right into it, allowing it to flame up and consume her.

"How dare you speak to her like that!" She stepped forward, putting a hand on Donna's shoulder. "She couldn't have known. You called her stupid, but you're the stupid one!"

"I beg your pardon!" The gentleman stepped back, eyebrows raised. "Are you raising your voice to me, child?" His eyes flashed dangerously, the softness gone.

"No, no, sir, no, she isn't, she isn't," said Mr. Thompson, hurrying over from his place by the cart. He put a soothing hand on the gentleman's arm. "You must forgive the child. She's not right in the head, you see."

He tapped his own cap conspiratorially. "Don't worry about her; and here's a bunch of mignonette for your troubles. They'll brighten your study right up, so they will, sir."

The gentleman seemed vaguely appeased. He melted off into the crowd, and Edith cringed, knowing what was coming. Already, she could hear Donna starting to sniffle as Mr. Thompson rounded on Edith.

"Speak to a customer like that again," he said coldly, "and you will be out of a job. Do you understand?"

Edith blinked back her tears. "Yes, sir," she whispered.

He gave her a long glare, but to her relief, he didn't seem inclined to reach for the cane this time. It had been a long week, and it seemed he was as ready to go home as the children were. "Well, turn out your pockets, then," he said, "and let's be done with it."

Edith felt a sinking sensation in the pit of her stomach. She set down her flowers in their basket and pulled a fistful of coins from her apron pocket.

Donna added hers, and they offered them to Mr. Thompson. The big man thumbed through them, his brow furrowed, his breathing loud and stertorous through chapped, swollen lips. Eventually, he picked out a few bits of money and flicked them into Donna's hand, then swept the rest of the money into his own pocket.

"There. That's yours," he said brusquely.

Edith stared at it in dismay, but she knew that arguing would do no good. Mr. Thompson had offered them only ten percent of what they sold, and he had given them exactly that amount. He was as good as his word, but she knew that they would be going hungry again tomorrow.

"Thank you, sir," she mumbled nonetheless.

The costermonger grunted and stumped off. Edith looked up at James, who had just lifted the handles of the cart. He gave her a painful attempt at a smile, his arms already trembling with the weight of the cart that he now had to push all the way to Mr. Thompson's house.

She wanted to smile back, but it was as though there were no smiles left inside her.

There was nothing at all but a Mama-shaped hole, and since Mama had been the world to Edith, that meant that her whole world was just an empty void.

Chapter Six

Three Years Later
1878

Edith had no idea where James was finding the strength to push the handcart. It had been such a long day, fighting so hard against the wind that even now blew in their faces as they headed up the street, the force of it so extreme that the three of them had to lean forward to make any progress at all.

James was moving at an agonized plod, his boots – oversized and gaping at the toes – slithering a little on the iced cobblestones with every step.

The handcart squeaked ahead of him, snow piling up on it as the wind drove it into their faces, its one sticky wheel making it almost impossible to push in a straight line.

Edith herself could hardly put one foot in front of the other, especially with Donna dragging so far behind her.

The little girl was only a touch bigger than she had been back in the dame school three years ago, but the weight of her hand in Edith's seemed immense. She dragged her feet, her head hanging, hair whipping neglected around her face.

Setting her head against the wind, Edith peered up the street. The dark gap of their alleyway was just a few more yards away. She took another step, and another. It didn't seem to be getting any closer, and the hill only seemed to grow steeper and steeper until it seemed as though she was climbing a vertical slope.

Vertical. That was a good word to remember; one of the words Mama had taught her, of what little she knew of mathematics and geometry. It was a little scandalous for a girl to know anything of those subjects at all, of course. But Mama had taught her everything she could.

The past tense came easier now. Mama was so very gone.

The dragging pull on Edith's arm became suddenly a dead weight, jerking her to a halt.

She almost cried; it felt as though momentum alone had been keeping her feet moving.

"Donna!" she groaned, looking back. "Come on. We're nearly there."

"Too tired," said Donna. She coughed painfully, dragged a ragged sleeve over her mouth. "I need a rest."

"You can rest when we're in the alley." Edith gave her arm another little tug. "It's too cold out here to stop now. Come on, Donnie. We're nearly there."

The little girl stumbled forward again, and somehow, a few minutes later, they had reached the alleyway between the old, ramshackle church and the back wall of a shop whose owner opened it too early and locked up too late to know that they slept there. James had beaten them there.

It wasn't much of a shelter; there was no roof, and snow still blew against the shop wall and then sludged its way down into the alley, but at least they were finally out of the wind. James had pushed the handcart up against the other side of the alley for a little shelter, and he was huddled up against it, striking a damp match with the slow, leaden movements of the utterly exhausted.

They had managed to scrounge a little coal today, and James managed to coax a tiny spark onto it. He shielded the fire from the wind with his body, blowing on it softly, his hands trembling with desperation.

Donna slumped to the ground between the growing fire and the handcart, saying nothing. She grasped one of the sacks they used as blankets and pulled it over her head, rolling herself into a ball.

Edith knew she should ask if Donna was hungry. The coal had cost them almost all their earnings for today, minus what they needed to keep for buying stock tomorrow, but she had a heel of bread wrapped in old newspapers in her apron pocket. But she didn't know which answer she feared most from the little girl: that she was hungry, or that she wasn't.

She sank down beside James, wordlessly digging out the bread and holding it out to him. He unwrapped it, broke it into three pieces; two slightly bigger, one very small.

"Here, Donnie, before you go to sleep," he said softly, putting a hand on Donna's shoulder. "Here's a little bread for you."

Donna rolled over to look up at James, her eyes rimmed with red. She sat up a little, wheezing with the effort, and took one of the larger pieces, nibbling on it without interest and pausing to cough at intervals.

James held the other larger piece out to Edith. "There you are," he said, with a brave effort at cheerfulness.

"Thank you." Edith took the piece of bread, hating herself for it a little but knowing that James would never accept it if she tried to give it back. She tore into it: it was the first she'd eaten all day, and she tried to chew it slowly, to make it last just a little longer. But it seemed to be gone in mere seconds.

Donna was still nibbling at hers, lying bundled up now, pausing at intervals just to breathe. James sat with one hand on her, stroking her shoulder. It seemed to take a mammoth effort for her to finish her bit of bread, and she fell asleep instantly, the sack pulled up over her shoulders.

"Poor mite," said James softly.

"She misses the house," said Edith. "She told me so."

"We all do, I think. But by the time we left..." James shook his head. "It was hardly any better than this alley anyway."

He was right, Edith knew. They had never had the money to care for the house, and Mama had barely had it either.

Years of neglect had all caught up with it last summer, when a sudden rainstorm had caused the roof to cave in. That had been the last straw.

They had tried huddling in the back corner of what had once been the classroom, where Edith and Mama had taught the children stories and rhymes and songs, but the rain had rotted the floor and everything had just been falling apart.

"I'm sorry we had to leave," said James, misreading her silence.

Edith shook her head. "Mr. Thompson was moving, too, not that it did him much good, poor old soul – considering he died just a few months after that. We didn't have a choice. And it's easier to stay near Covent Garden, for the flowers, and…" She felt her cheeks flush, ashamed of the truth. "I wanted to leave. I don't miss the house. It wasn't home anymore… not without…" She couldn't say *Mama* out loud.

James put an arm around her shoulders, and she leaned against him. His presence was doing something a little different to her these days, something she couldn't quite define. Maybe it had something to do with the way her body was changing, her hips widening just a fraction as her body strove to leave girlhood behind despite the fact that it received barely enough food to live at all.

Either way, it was one of the few good – if confusing – things in her life, and she allowed herself to rest her head on his chest and listen to the steady thump of his heart.

"It's almost Christmas," he said. "People are going to start buying more things now, you'll see. And then it will be a little easier."

Edith managed not to flinch over the word *Christmas*, even though all of her wanted to. She tilted her head back, looking up into James' eyes to keep from crying.

He grinned at her, as though Christmas still held something for him, something a tiny bit special.

The magic was all gone for Edith. But there was still something in his eyes that made her remember, at least, that there had been magic once, before Mama died and the world lost all of its colour.

"Maybe," she murmured.

"You know it will." James gave her shoulders a gentle squeeze. "Rest now, Edie. It's all right. I'm here."

She closed her eyes. Nothing was all right, but at least James was here. And that was the only thing that made it all tolerable: the way the wind shrieked past the alley mouth, the way the snow slid off the rooftops and onto the handcart in the middle of the night, the ache of hunger in her belly, the harsh crackle of Donna's breathing.

At least James was here. That was all she had left.

~ ~ ~ ~ ~

Edith tried not to spit the word *Christmas* as though it was acid. Holding up a handful of hateful, hateful mistletoe, she plastered a manufactured smile onto her face, calling out to the passers-by on this busy little thoroughfare near Covent Garden.

"Lovely Christmas!" she called out. "Pretty Christmas for your homes! It's not too early to get started on your decorations!"

"Holly and mistletoe!" Donna chimed in beside her. She paused, letting out a painful cough. "Perfect for wreaths!"

How was it fair that there were people thinking about ribbons and wreaths and Christmas trees, while Donna shivered on the street beside Edith?

The little girl's nose was running, and she kept wiping it on her sleeve, but it was driving people away nonetheless.

Potential customers would come a little nearer, then shy away and give the child a wide berth. And maybe they wouldn't think about her again at all.

Maybe they really just didn't care that there were innocent little children like Donna – sweet Donna, or at least, she had been sweet once, before all this – suffering on the streets in the harsh belly of midwinter.

All they could think about was pretty, happy, jolly Christmas, and not the vicious bite of the wind or the cruelty of the early nightfall or how very long and very dark the mornings were when the coals began to burn very low.

She forced herself to swallow that bitterness and took a step forward.

Standing right on the curb she shouted "Evergreens! Evergreens. Get your lovely Christmas evergreens!"

A cab rattled past, the sodden horse shaking his ears against the snow, and Edith spotted the puddle in the gutter a second too late.

She jumped back, but the wheel still rushed right through the puddle, spraying slush up against her knees.

She gave a little yelp of dismay. In this weather, her dress would take days to dry out, and already she could feel the damp chill against her shins.

"Oh, poor Edie," said Donna softly.

Edith forced a smile for her. "It's all right," she said. "This bit of holly got wet, too. Let me walk back to the cart and put it away where it'll dry off."

She would give any excuse to go back to the cart, truth be told.

Leaving Donna on the corner, Edith crossed the street carefully to where James was standing with the handcart. Even from several yards away, she could see his bright, dazzling smile.

His golden hair was a splash of colour on the grey street, and his voice lent colour to the air as well, like music threading its way through the buzz and rumble of the streets.

He was singing. "The holly bears a bark as bitter as any gall; and Mary bore sweet Jesus Christ for to redeem us all. The rising of the sun, and the running of the deer, the playing of the merry organ, sweet singing in the choir."

Edith thought to herself that no choir in the world could equal the simple purity of James' own singing voice. It had a fine, deep timbre to it nowadays that sent a little shiver down her spine as she approached him.

He was singing the last stanza of his Christmas carol, gesturing at the holly he'd used to decorate his handcart and holding up handfuls of oranges to the people passing by.

It was unsurprising when a woman in a housekeeper's uniform stepped out of the crowd, purse in hand. "What a sweet voice you have, young man," she said.

"Thank you, ma'am, but not quite so sweet as yours." James doffed his cap briskly, his cheerful patter flowing effortlessly from him. "And neither are my oranges; but it would be hard to match a lady's voice like yours for sweetness, so perhaps you'd still give them a chance."

Flattered, the housekeeper laughed. "Well, I suppose I shall have to try them," she said. "Give me half-a-dozen."

"How about seven for the price of six?" said James, with a bright smile. "Why, you'll save tuppence."

"Then that's all fine," said the housekeeper, and tipped the coins into his palm, "but I'll pay you for seven if you'll give me another song."

James laughed, doffing his cap again. "Which would be your pleasure, ma'am?"

"Do you know 'Good King Wenceslas'?" asked the housekeeper.

"Indeed I do!" said James, and launched heartily into the carol.

It was a favourite of Mama's, and Edith listened to it with a steady, dull bitterness rising in her heart. She had always loved it when she was a little girl. Now, however, it all rang with such falseness. The thought that a king, with access to flesh and wine and pine logs, would trek through the freezing cold to give food and drink and warmth to some poor peasant – it was mere foolishness.

None of the rich folk that Edith sold flowers to every day would ever have dreamed of going a single step out of their way to help her, or anyone.

"Therefore, Christian men be sure, wealth or rank possessing: ye, who now will bless the poor will yourselves find blessing," James sang, giving the last note a little flourish.

"Indeed one will, young man," said the housekeeper. "Have a merry Christmas, and thank you for the oranges and the song."

"Thank you for listening, ma'am," said James, with another winning smile.

The housekeeper went her way, and Edith came up to James, laying her wet holly in the cart and looking for a dry sprig. "If only King Wenceslas was real," she sighed.

"I think he was, but it was a long time ago," said James. "Are you all right? You're all wet."

"I'm all right," lied Edith. "I've sold three bunches of holly, and one of mistletoe."

"Wonderful!" James beamed, laying a hand on her shoulder. "That's good news, Edie. See? Christmas will be good to us after all."

Across the street, some men were busy setting up a Christmas tree outside a bakery. It was just a bare pine tree now, but Edith knew that in a few days, it would be all hung with ribbons and candy. The sight made her feel sick. She turned away.

"It's just you, who is good, James," she said, "no one else in this world is good, no one else even sees us here, shivering and starving."

James lowered his hand to his side again. "I'm sorry," he offered softly.

"None of it is your fault. I just want Christmas to be over," said Edith, her bitterness burning at the back of her throat. "And I want all these rich folks with their stupid trees and cards and presents to give their money to people like us instead."

"They're buying our evergreens," said James gently. "That helps us."

Edith shook her head. She didn't want to hear it, any of it; in fact, she didn't even know if she wanted the rich to give their Christmas money to the poor.

She just didn't want Christmas to happen at all, to anyone, ever. It was all such a sham. It was all so empty.

"Edie." James touched her arm. "I'm here for you. It's you and me and Donna, always."

She looked up at him, and the same hope that had been in his voice as he sang about Good King Wenceslas gleamed in his eyes. She tried to cling to it, searching his face, looking for the secret way in which he could somehow hold on to the magic when it was all gone for her.

"Thank you," she murmured, then turned and headed back to her miserable corner, a fresh bunch of holly clutched in her hands.

~ ~ ~ ~ ~

Edith wasn't sure if Donna felt warm, or if her own hands were just terribly cold. She tucked the sack around the sleeping child's shoulders, grateful at least that she'd eaten her gruel.

"Is she asleep?" asked James, who was melting some snow in their dented pan over the fire.

"Yes, and she seems to be sleeping soundly," said Edith. She sat down beside him.

He gave her a worried look. "Did she seem a little hot to you?"

"Maybe," said Edith. "I don't know."

James ran a worried hand through his hair. "She was coughing more today. I don't know what's the matter with her..." He gave Edith an agonized look. "She's not even excited for Christmas at all. She's always excited for Christmas."

"She'll be so glad when you give her that bit of Christmas money you've been saving for her," said Edith.

James touched her arm. "Thank you, Edie. It was so kind of you to agree that I could keep a few pennies aside to get her something for Christmas. I just want to see her happy again... even if it's only for a moment."

"Of course. You're right," said Edith. "And it is a better time of the year right now, when people are buying evergreens and feeling a little more generous."

It would be followed, Edith knew, by one of the coldest, harshest, and sparsest times of the year for people like her and the Walshes.

The bitter cold of January, with that so-called "Christmas spirit" would soon all be gone and strip away the fake generosity of the rich.

There would be no seasonal flowers available, and no need for anyone to buy evergreens. This was the season when they would try to sell hothouse flowers then, which cost a fortune.

"Maybe I should tell her that I'm going to get her a little treat for Christmas," said James. "Maybe then she'll feel better."

"Maybe," said Edith.

James gave her a sidelong look, then reached into the pocket of his tattered coat. "I have *your* Christmas present," he said. "I know it's a few days early, but I can't keep it – it'll be damaged. And not very up to date."

"James!" Edith felt a tiny spark of excitement despite herself. "What are you talking about?"

He grinned at her, and something bright glittered in his eyes, raising her spirits for a precious moment. Drawing something out of his pocket, he held it out to her. "Merry Christmas," he said softly.

Edith gasped. Reaching forward slowly and carefully, she closed her fingers around a crisp, brand-new newspaper. The date on the front page was today, and even by the pathetic glow of their tiny fire, the words were effortless to read.

NEWCASTLE INVENTOR ANNOUNCES INCANDESCENT LIGHT BULB.

The print so clear, so perfect. Edith ran a forefinger over the page, almost expecting it to still be warm from the press. Tears built in her eyes.

They had had to sell all of Mama's books, even *Moby-Dick*, in their efforts to survive.

Ever since, she had clung to her literacy by reading scraps of old newspapers by the poor firelight.

It was difficult, and papers were hard to come by, much less papers that were legible at all; it had been months since she'd been able to read an entire article without any of the words being torn out or blurred by staining or damp.

"A whole paper?" she breathed.

"I wanted a book, but they were too expensive." James blushed. "I hope it's all right."

"Oh, James, it's perfect." Edith looked up at him. "Thank you. I don't know how you did it."

"Donna helped. She wanted you to have it," said James. "Maybe you'll read some to her?" His eyes were pleading.

"Of course I will." Edith hesitated. "I... I have been trying to teach her, you know."

"I know," said James quickly. "She's just too tired when we get back from a day on the streets, these days. That's not your fault." He laid a hand on her arm. "I just think she'd like to hear about the... the new light bulb, I think?"

"That's right!" Edith grinned at him.

"They're the only two words I could read in the headline." James laughed. "Don't be too impressed."

"But I *am* impressed." Edith smiled. "I know we haven't worked much on reading, and you got a late start. But you're doing well, James. You really are."

"I have a good teacher." James winked. "That first word – it looked like a town's name I've seen on signs before. New... something."

"Newcastle," said Edith.

"That's it. And the second one? In..."

"Take your time." Edith spread the paper over James' lap, where the light was better.

"Sound each letter out slowly." The words spilled out of her mouth easily, as though the past three years had never happened, and she was back in the dame school teaching the children how to read. More than that, she could hear the echo of her mother's voice through her own as she spoke.

She clung to that echo, shuffling a little closer to James. He'd always been so grateful as she'd taught him how to read over the past few years, but he didn't know that teaching him – and reading herself – was her only connection to her happier past. More than that, it felt like her only connection to her future, too: that bright future that Mama had promised her, because of her education.

James stared at the word, his eyes intent. "In... ven... tor," he said. "Inventor?"

"That's right!" Edith leaned her head against his shoulder. "Now, let's try the next word."

She stayed close to James, feeling his voice rumble through him as he eagerly started sounding out one syllable at a time. Mama had been wrong about Christmas and its magic. All the magic had been inside her.

But Edith could still cling to the hope that Mama had been right about another thing: that education, somehow, would give them a better future.

Chapter Seven

Christmas Eve was clear for once, and not windy, but somehow it seemed even colder for it. Every surface glittered with the thick snow that had fallen in the night.

The twilit sky, as black and purple as a bruise, was dotted with a handful of distant stars; their light achieved nothing but to stir sad longing in Edith's heart as she looked up at them. Mama had loved the stars.

It was almost impossible to stop thinking about Mama tonight. Not with the bright Christmas tree standing right beside the bakery. This one had an angel on the top with a white silk dress, shimmering in the glow of the streetlamp nearby.

It was covered in red ribbons. The sight of them sickened Edith, making them remember all too well the day that that red ribbon had come loose in the breeze and drifted out into the street, luring Donna into the path of the speeding cab that had killed Mama.

She glanced over at Donna, who was wilting beside her, sorrowfully and silently holding up her bunches of holly to the muffled strangers passing by. The bitter cold had turned Donna's lips blue, and goosebumps were visible on her hands as she held them up.

No one paid her any mind; everyone was too busy hurrying home to whatever warmth, food, and companionship awaited them on Christmas Eve. People only saw the ones they knew or were meeting up with, and cries of "Merry Christmas!" rang around the street.

Merry. How could people say that? Edith was appalled at their heartlessness.

She and Donna were standing right there, cold and starving, her grief like a boulder in her chest. How could people say "merry"? She just wanted Christmas to be over.

"Edie," said Donna faintly.

Edith looked down. The child's face was deathly pale. "What is it, dear?" she asked.

Donna turned her face up towards Edith. She was unrecognizable as the child who had run into the streets three years ago today, the child whose happy face was forever frozen in Edith's memory.

Her eyes were larger and more solemn than ever now, and they were set in a grey face, pinched with starvation, her hair limp and filthy where it hung around her cheeks.

"I... I don't feel well," she whispered.

"It's nearly time to go home, Donnie," said Edith, not knowing what else to say. She felt helpless rage swamp her. She so wanted to be able to help Donna somehow, but there was nothing she could do. Nothing.

"I don't…" Donna wobbled on her feet. With a faint slap, her holly bunches fell to the ground.

"Donna?" Edith turned to her.

Donna raised a hand to her head and gave a tiny, soft whimper.

Then her knees buckled underneath her, and she fell to the ground with a quiet thump.

"Donna!" Edith flung down her own evergreens and fell to her knees beside the little girl, grasping at her shoulders. They were skeletal against her fingers. "Donna. Donna! Wake up!"

Her cries rang around the street, drawing a crowd of people who started to shout advice. "Slap her face. Shake her," said one old woman.

Pedestrians started shoving at the crowd, trying to get past; one of them tripped over Edith's feet, their shoes trampling painfully on her ankles, but she had eyes only for Donna's ashen face and closed eyes.

She fell desperately to the ground, pressing her ear against the little girl's chest. To her terrified relief, she heard wheezing, crackling breaths and the thud-thud-thud-thud of a little heart.

"Get some water!" shouted a gruff old gentleman. "It'll soon snap her out of it."

"Have you gone mad, sir?" cried Edith, looking over her shoulder at him. "She'll catch her death!"

His eyes narrowed at her impudent tone. "Seems to me she's already caught it," he sniffed, stalking away.

No. Those words couldn't be true. Edith clutched at Donna's hands; they were like ice. "Donnie, wake up," she begged. "Donna, come on!"

"Donnie!" James' cry was a terrible, panicked wail of fear. He shoved through the crowd, flinging himself to his knees beside Donna, grabbing at her arms. "What happened?"

"I don't know." Tears started to flow helplessly down Edith's cheeks. "She just… fainted."

"Donna, come on, come on, wake up." James grabbed the child, pulling her limp body against his chest. "Come on, Donnie. Wake up for me."

Suddenly, life seemed to return to the little girl. Her limbs twitched, and she gave a long moan, her eyelids fluttering.

"That's right! Wake up," cried Edith, rubbing her back vigorously. "Wake up."

"Jimmy?" Donna's eyes fluttered open, focusing briefly on her brother.

"It's all right. I'm right here." James held her close to his chest, rising to his feet. He gazed around at the crowd in bewilderment, tears glittering on his cheeks, his nose blue with cold. No one said anything; everyone was just staring. "She needs a doctor," he croaked out at last. "Please. Does anyone know a doctor? I can pay. I have money."

Edith scoffed. None of these people would help at all, she knew it. But to her surprise, the old woman who had suggested the slapping stepped forward. "If you go to the end of the street, then turn left, you'll find Dr. Finley's house," she said. "He'll help you, young man. Go quickly. She doesn't look like she has much time."

"Thank you. Thank you." James' eyes found Edith. "You'll stay with the handcart?"

It was the last thing she wanted to do. She didn't dare to let James and Donna out of her sight right now, but that cart was their survival, so she stood watching him run down the street with Donna's limp little figure in his arms, her head on his shoulder, and her little feet sticking out over his arm, flopping lifelessly with every stride.

~ ~ ~ ~ ~

It grew late, then even later. Edith, not knowing what else to do, eventually pushed the handcart back to the alley. It was only two blocks, but in the bitter cold with her body so spent by worry and weeping, it took her more than an hour.

The handcart seemed to weigh as much as the world, and she struggled up the hill with it. Her tears grew cold on her cheeks. She pushed it a few feet, then stopped, bracing a shoulder against it to keep it from rolling, and sucked in agonizing breaths of the freezing air. Then pushed again. A few feet at a time.

It was all too heavy for her. Why was it all so heavy?

At last, Edith reached the alleyway. She shoved the handcart up against a wall and collapsed, exhausted, by their fireplace.

There had been two coals left over from last night's fire, but someone had stolen them. She sat with her arms around her knees, staring dully at the empty spot, before she realized that she would die of cold if she just sat here.

So she struggled to her feet and stumbled back to the marketplace to see if she could find any kind of fuel for the few pennies she had in her pocket from the day's sales.

She eventually scrounged a few sticks of half-dry driftwood from a rag-and-bone man who was trying to get to sleep under a bench, and by the time she had coaxed those pathetic sticks into burning, it was very late. The bell tolled midnight: it was Christmas Day now. Another Christmas Day that Mama was dead.

Maybe Donna was dead too. And James. And everything.

The terrible thought had just seized her limbs when she heard the soft tread of feet in the mouth of the alleyway. She lunged to her feet, but it was James, and he was carrying Donna in his arms. Her face had a little more colour in it, and she seemed to be sleeping peacefully.

"James." Edith hurried to him, wrapped her arms around them both, and held them for a long moment. James leaned into her, resting his head on her shoulder as though his strength was utterly spent.

He had never done that before. Somehow, it gave her strength of her own, although she didn't know where it had come from.

"Did you find the doctor?" she asked, stepping back and looking down at Donna's sleeping face.

"Yes. He gave her some medicine, to help her sleep." James staggered over to the fire and lay Donna down on a few old rags beside it, then spread her sack over her, pausing to tuck a strand of her oily hair behind her ear.

Edith didn't dare to ask what was wrong with her. James sank down by the fire and sat there for a few long moments, just staring at the little flames.

"Could... could you pay him?" she said at last, more to break the silence than because of anything else.

"Yes. The money I was saving for Donna for Christmas... he said it was enough. He was kind." James let out a long, shuddering breath, then looked up at Edith. "But oh, Edie... it's consumption."

The word struck a cold lance down into the very pit of Edith's stomach.

She remembered the first time she'd heard it, when another doctor, years ago, had come to see Papa where he lay coughing and wheezing in the same bed she'd shared with Mama. *Consumption.* The way he'd said it had been like the slamming of a door, and a few short days later, Papa was gone.

"But she seems better now," Edith protested. "She... she's quieter."

"It's the medicine. But I could only get enough for tonight. She needs more medicine, and food, and... and she needs to be out of the wind and wet."

James rested a hand on Donna's shoulder, as he always did in the evenings as they sat talking around the fire.

"Maybe we can go back to the house," said Edith desperately.

"Edie, it's too far and what is the good of it anyway?. It was falling down and caved in when we left it, it can't offer us any better shelter than the alleys." James wiped at his eyes. "There's only one thing that I can do for her now, Edie."

Edith felt ice cold. "What?"

He looked up at her, and the resolve in his eyes was as steely as it was painful. "I can take her to the workhouse," he said.

"The workhouse!" Edith flew to her feet. "James, you can't, you can't!"

There had been children in the dame school who had told stories of being in the workhouse when their families had fallen on hard times.

The stories they had told had been terrifying: the bullies, the pitiful allowance of food, the punishments, the utter loneliness and misery of it all.

Mama had always said that nothing could be worse than a workhouse for a little child. Nothing at all.

"I have to," said James.

"But James, she'll be taken away from you," said Edith. "You won't be able to go and visit her. It will be as though she's in prison."

"I know." James looked up at her. "That's why I'm going into the workhouse, too."

Edith felt as though the world had suddenly crumbled under her, the earth become void underneath her feet. "They'll separate you," she cried. "You'll be put in with the men, and she'll be with the girls younger than fourteen, and – "

"And you'd be with the women," said James. "But at least we'd be in the same building, Edie. And we wouldn't have to find a way to get money to buy flowers… and if we were sick, they would at least give us medicine. And Donna will sleep in the warm and dry, every single night." His eyes were pleading. "Don't you understand?"

"Mama always said there was nothing worse than a workhouse," said Edith, wiping at her eyes.

"Your mama never slept a night of her life on the street," snapped James.

Edith felt as though he'd punched her in the belly. She leaned back, wide-eyed and horrified that he would say such a thing. He realized his mistake immediately, grabbing her hand, his eyes softening. "Edie – I'm sorry. I didn't mean it like that."

"Then how did you mean it, James?" she demanded, everything in her hurting. "Did you mean that my mama was wrong?"

"I loved your mama. She was like the mama I never had," said James gently. "But is there really nothing worse than the workhouse? Donna will be safe there, Edie."

He paused, his eyes growing pained. "The doctor said that it's her only chance of surviving the winter. I have to take that chance. No matter if it means separation from her. I just have to do whatever it takes… whatever it takes to save her."

Edith stared at him. Maybe he was right, but all she could think of was how Mama would feel if she knew Edith was in a workhouse, especially over Christmas. She'd be stuffed into a terrible, ugly, striped uniform, and treated as both a prisoner and a slave. And she'd have no chance of seeing James, no say in how her day would go, no chance of making her own money or finding that better future that Mama had always spoken of. That future on which Mama had placed all of her hope.

Besides that, she didn't think she could face the thought of being so brutally separated from James and Donna, and thrust into a dormitory with hundreds of other women. The stories she had heard of the way people treated one another in that workhouse... it was too much to bear. She would rather take her chances on the street.

"Please, Edie." James' face was crumpling with emotion. "Say something."

"I can't." Edith dropped her eyes to the ground. "I can't go into the workhouse, James."

There was a moment of silence between them. She had felt many silences between her and James before: the contented quiet as they sat together by the fire, the mutual desperation as they strove side by side. But this was different. This silence stretched between them like a barred gate.

"I understand that," said James quietly. "You can read and write, and you have skills that your mama taught you. You can find work – good work. You can improve your station in life." He reached for her hands, but even his touch felt different. "I just don't have that choice."

"Let Donna go to the workhouse," said Edith desperately. "You and I can go on selling things, and we'll go get her in the summer, when…"

"Edie." James squeezed her hands. "You know I can't do that. I can't leave her there. I know we'll be separated, but at least we'll be in the same building." His eyes implored her to understand.

She knew she should understand. She knew she could, if she tried, but she didn't want to; she didn't want to understand that he had to go.

That he was going to be torn from her arms, just like Mama and Papa.

"Please, Edie." James bit his lip. "I don't want to leave you."

"Then don't." Edith pulled her hands from his grip.

"Edie…"

She ignored him, hating herself for it, but so torn and confused and weighed down by grief that she hardly knew what else to do. She wrapped herself around Donna, the way she slept every night, and pulled a sack over her shoulders. Then she cuddled close into the little girl, burying her face in the grubby hair that smelled like medicine now instead of like Donna, and wept.

She knew that James loved her, but she also knew that he loved Donna more than anything in the world. And she knew that this would be the last night that she would have company in this alleyway.

~ ~ ~ ~ ~

The workhouse had made an effort to decorate for Christmas, and somehow that made it all the more grotesque and appalling. It was a tall building, all sheer brick and small windows, with high walls and barred gates all around.

There was a grim air about it, something harsh and cruel that seeped out of the very bricks from which it was built. It crept under Edith's skin, an insidious chill that froze her bones, and the holly wreaths on the doors and candles in the windows only accentuated it.

The little wreaths and small strings of bunting were so pitiful against the austerity of the workhouse that it only made it all the more obvious and glaring.

Donna sat on her brother's hip like a toddler, her legs dangling limply from under her filthy dress, her eyes listless as she cradled her head on his shoulder. "What is this place, Jimmy?" she whimpered.

James kissed her forehead. His hands were shaking, and Edith could hear the tears in his voice. "It's... a sort of hospital, Donnie," he told her. "You're going to get better in here. And get something nice for Christmas, too. And make lots and lots of new friends your age, and get back to your learning, too. Wouldn't that be nice?"

Donna seemed too tired and sick to care. She closed her eyes, leaning into James' neck again.

They had walked up to the gate now, and they could see through the iron bars to the tall, narrow door. There was a wreath hanging on it; it was sadly wilted, the edges crumpled, and very small compared to the vast and stern facade of the building.

James stopped, turning to face Edith. The tears were spilling over now, coursing clean lines down his dirty cheeks.

"You can still come with us," he said quietly, fighting for control over his voice.

Edith couldn't be angry with him, not now, but neither could she step through that gate and walk up to that terrible doorway. She had to find another way. He had given her the last of his money, for buying flowers. It would work. It would be better than this.

"You can still stay," she whispered.

His arms tightened around little Donna, who was almost comatose on his shoulder now, her little head lolling.

"I can't," he said. "Even though I want to." He turned as if to go, and then hesitated. "Maybe she'll be better in the summer. She'll be better, and we... we'll find you again."

The falter in his voice belied the fact that even he hardly believed his words, but Edith clutched at them. She had nothing else to hold on to, after all.

"I'll find you," she whispered.

He stepped forward, his warmth enfolding her, and bent down to kiss her delicately on the forehead. He had never kissed her before, and the kiss awoke something in her that she had never felt before. She leaned into it, but it was over and he was stepping back and turning away.

"Goodbye, Edie," he croaked.

As he walked up to the gate and rang the bell, the sound seemed to wake Donna. She raised her head, blinking at James.

"Goodbye?" she mumbled. "Why are we saying goodbye? Isn't Edie coming with us?"

"No, pet," said James. "But it's all right. We'll see her again when you're all better."

"But why isn't she coming?" Donna's voice rose, raw and painful, but terrified.

A porter had come out of the workhouse now and was opening the gate, regarding James with bitter indifference. Tears coursed down Edith's cheeks as James stepped through that gate. It slammed behind him with an iron sound, a final sound.

"We'll see her again," James was saying, his voice cracking.

They had reached the door. The porter barred their way. "Put the girl down. She goes to a separate room."

"Separate?" Donna clutched at James. "Jimmy, no! Jimmy, don't let me go! Don't let me go!"

Her shrieks reverberated around the building, and Edith couldn't stand it, because her own heart was screaming the same thing. She turned and fled into the silent streets and the cold emptiness of Christmas Eve.

~ ~ ~ ~ ~

Edith had never been so cold before. Every part of her was shivering when she awoke, and she ached; at least, parts of her ached. Other parts – her fingers and toes, her left cheek where it pressed against the cold dirt – had gone completely numb. They felt as though they no longer belonged to her.

She welcomed the numbness. It was better than the pain. It was better than love, or hope, or magic. It was better than anything.

There was sunlight, so it must be day, and that meant work. For the first time in years, Edith wasn't hungry, but she knew she needed to eat.

To do that, she needed to sell flowers. This was a fact she could cling to, and it drove her to her feet and out of the alleyway.

She was at the back gate of Covent Garden when she realized that it was Christmas Day, and there would be no one there to sell cut flowers to her.

She was right: the gate was shut up fast, and Christmas decorations were everywhere, with hothouse flowers adorning them and evergreen wreaths hanging from every surface.

Evergreens. Edith's stomach lurched. She still had some evergreens, she realized. She'd put them in the handcart two days ago, when James had taken Donna to the doctor. She could sell those.

The thought of holding those things in her hands, those useless, senseless symbols of a joyous hope that no longer existed for Edith, was sickening.

But in the same moment she realized that it had been two days since she'd last eaten, and so she had no choice.

She picked her way back to the alley, stumbling over each step, and retrieved what little of her merchandise was left. They were starting to dry up, but they would have to do.

Making her way to the thoroughfare where she usually had her best business, Edith stepped out onto her usual corner only to stand still in shock. It took her a few moments, again, to realize what was happening.

The street was absolutely empty except for the wreaths and bunting that hung from the lampposts, and for the Christmas tree on the bakery corner, with its angel's white silk robe fluttering in the cold wind.

Of course. No one was here either, because it was Christmas Day, and everyone was inside with food and family and presents and decorations.

Edith's limbs failed her. She crumpled down onto the empty pavement, clutching her wilted evergreens to her chest.

Through the blurry veil of tears, she gazed around at the city where it slumbered beneath its blankets of snow.

The sky was the colour of metal, heavy and unyielding, pressing down on her; there were pools of golden light coming from the windows of the little flats above the shops, and she could hear bursts of music and laughter coming from them as people enjoyed the festive day together.

People who still believed in Christmas magic, and who hadn't seen it so completely broken. People who had experienced more than just loss, cold, hunger and loneliness on Christmas Day.

The snow began to fall. Perhaps, from inside those golden windows, it looked beautiful: the shimmering snowflakes tumbling down and coating every decoration with a fine dust of glittering white.

But Edith felt only the cold on her face, on her eyelashes, and knew that now there was no chance of anyone coming by to purchase some last-minute evergreens for their table.

For Edith, the snow, like Christmas, was nothing but suffering upon suffering.

Chapter Eight

New Year's Day had come and gone. Edith could count on the fingers of both hands how many times she'd had something to eat between Christmas Day and now, and she would have fingers left over, too.

She was trying not to think about this as she walked through the teeming crowds at Covent Garden Market. T

here were grand terraces here, and wing upon wing of great buildings where rich folk bought orchids and exotic flowers whose names Edith didn't even know.

Instead, she was heading around the back of the market, where smaller stallholders set up ramshackle little stands and sold mostly fruit and vegetables.

There was one old man, however, who sold flowers from the hothouses inside Covent Garden, and it was for his stall that Edith headed. She had to twist and push through the crowd as she went. No one seemed interested in stepping out of the way of a girl in a ragged dress.

A few men spat and cursed at her, and the slightly better-off ladies gave her arrogant glares as she passed.

At last, she reached the stall that was tucked away around the corner of one of the buildings.

She always had the sense that perhaps old Mr. Garrett wasn't meant to be selling these hothouse flowers, and that perhaps they were smuggled out of the hothouses without anyone knowing; he seemed to work as a gardener here, selling his flowers after hours and on weekends.

But they were cheap. Edith didn't have the money to be asking questions.

Mr. Garrett, a bent little old figure, was silently packing a few little pots into a box. Standing on the other side of his rickety table was a short, squat older woman of preposterous proportions. Edith didn't think she'd ever seen someone with a face so pinched, shoulders so narrow, and hips quite so wide before.

The older lady stood with her arms folded, the lines of her face all pointing straight down, with angry folds around her faded eyes and jowly mouth as she glared soundlessly at Mr. Garrett.

Edith couldn't help but feel a pang of jealousy as she stopped a few feet away, awaiting her turn. The woman had a little handcart beside her. It was nothing like the clumsy costermonger's cart, which served Edith now only as a windbreak, and not a very good one: it was simply too heavy for her to push every day.

This woman's cart, however, was made of wicker with nice big wheels, and it looked easy to push. Right now, it was laden with potted flowers, too – a far better and easier way to make money. Potted flowers could survive for weeks if you could just water them, and that was easy enough. They didn't wilt in a single day like cut flowers did, but Edith could never afford them.

She watched with growing envy as the root-seller packed the pots into her basket and counted out some money for Mr. Garrett, then paused to contemplate the cut flowers he was displaying in bunches on the other side of the table.

There were only a few bunches of wallflowers, Edith noted with rising panic in her heart. She'd always had good luck selling mignonettes, but ever since a new costermonger had moved into her area, she'd been forced to wander to different areas because everyone was more willing to buy from this better-dressed man than from Edith. And in her new area, wallflowers were her best sellers.

Exhaustion sucked at her limbs. She had a long way to walk from here to start selling, and even longer to walk back to the alley. Truth be told, it was impractical to sleep in that alley anymore, but she couldn't leave it. It was close to the workhouse.

She stepped forward, desperate. She needed those wallflowers. "Mr. Garrett, sir, good morning," she quavered. "If you please, I need some wallflowers."

Mr. Garrett gave her a silent, morose look. The root-seller rounded on her, planting her small hands on her wide hips.

She hesitated for a second as her eyes rested on Edith's, and for a moment, Edith almost expected her to be kind. But of course, that was not the case.

"Mr. Garrett is busy serving me now, you young hussy," she snapped. "Wait your turn."

"If you please, ma'am." Edith swallowed tears of desperation and tiredness. "I just need some wallflowers."

"Perhaps I need some wallflowers, too," said the woman angrily.

"But you have roots," said Edith, helpless rage rising in her. "Look at all those pretty potted moss-roses and fuchsias. Please – I don't have money for roots. I just want some cut flowers, and I need wallflowers."

"Then you'll have to go somewhere else to get them," said the root-seller spitefully. She swept the wallflowers into her hands. "I'll take all of these, Mr. Garrett."

Edith stared at the woman, her heart shattering around her feet. Now she would need to walk all the way to Farringdon, nearly two miles away, to buy her flowers – then all the way in the other direction to sell them.

"Please," she choked, tears filling her eyes.

"Be off with you!" The woman flapped a hand impatiently. "I don't have time for your fuss."

Mr. Garrett gave her a warning look, and Edith knew that this root-seller must support him far more with buying his pots than Edith did with buying a few sad little bunches each day. The tears spilled over as she turned and moved away, pushing blindly through the crowd.

It was beginning to look like she would have no choice but to leave the workhouse behind and move closer to Farringdon. But how could she?

~ ~ ~ ~ ~

By that Sunday morning, Edith still hadn't made up her mind, but she knew that something would have to change. Her limbs were throbbing as she plodded down the street, her eyes feeling like they'd been filled with sand. Even the nice weather could do nothing to raise her spirits: there was no wind, and balmy sunshine poured richly down into the street, filled with the tolling of church bells.

There would be no one to sell flowers to until around eleven or twelve o' clock, when people started leaving church to go home. That was why Edith's feet were carrying her to the workhouse.

She knew that she had to change something. Selling flowers all the way on the edge of Whitechapel – where barely anyone bought anything; but at least there were no other flower-sellers to compete with – while buying them at Covent Garden and visiting the workhouse in Mayfair was just too much.

And while her mind was telling her to move towards Whitechapel and buy her flowers at Farringdon, Edith's heart wouldn't let go of the workhouse.

It wouldn't let go of James.

The porter was standing outside today, smoking a pipe as he gazed listlessly into the street. Edith went up to the gate and stood there for a few moments.

His eyes rested on her, but he made no effort to speak to her or come nearer, so eventually she called out to him.

"Sir, I do beg your pardon, but might you be of assistance?"

The porter raised an eyebrow, chuckling. "Think you're all high-born today, do you?" he grunted.

Edith had hoped that her educated tone would earn his respect, but it seemed that she was incapable of this. "If you please, sir," she said, "all I want is to speak to a friend of mine who's in here."

The porter took his pipe out of his mouth and gave her a long, steely glare. "Do you want to be admitted to the workhouse?"

"No!" cried Edith, backing away.

"Then go away." The porter returned his pipe to his mouth. "This is a workhouse, not a hotel, ain't it? Be off with you."

"Sir, please. He's the only friend I have," Edith began.

The porter rolled his eyes. "I'll make it clear for you, you stupid girl," he said. "Be gone, or I'll set the dogs on you."

Edith backed away, heartbroken and confused. Mama had been right about the workhouse after all. This was no haven for the poverty-stricken – it was a prison.

She walked away, following the wall of the workhouse until it became the iron bars of one of the work-yards outside. She'd seen these yards before, filled with people all in the same uniform, working away at monotonous tasks: hanging washing, picking oakum, shelling peas.

This yard was filled with young men, and they were all armed with a hammer and chisel, breaking up big rocks into smaller and smaller ones.

Young men. Edith stopped, her heart suddenly thundering. Maybe James was in here, and even though the thought of him in this prison broke her heart, she still pressed herself up against the bars and eagerly searched the rows of uniforms, hoping desperately that he might be there.

And he was. And not far away, either. Just a stone's throw on the other side of the bars, James sat with a hammer in his hand, slowly breaking up a big stone into little chunks. She could tell from the way he moved that he was tired, from the way that his shoulders slouched that he was defeated; but just the sight of him was enough to set her heart racing with relief. It was as though the sunshine suddenly shone on her for the first time all day.

"James!" she cried.

His head snapped up at once. He looked around, and his eyes found hers. Instantly, he was on his feet, rushing to her, seizing her hands through the bars, pushing his arms through to wrap them around her and laugh and cry as he clutched at her. It was uncomfortable to be pressed against the bars like this, but Edith leaned into them, weeping with joy as she clung to him.

"Oh, Edie, Edie, how I've missed you. How glad I am that you came to see me!" James pulled back, staring at her as though she was the only thing in the world. "I thought you were cross... I thought you'd never come."

"Of course I came," said Edith. She clutched at his hands. "I'm not angry. I – I just miss you."

"I miss you, too," said James. "Have they told you anything about Donna?"

Edith stared at him. "No. Have they told you nothing?"

"Nothing." James' eyes filled with tears. "They won't tell me a thing... not a thing." He wiped at them angrily. "And you? Are you all right? You're so thin... you look so tired."

"I'm all right," said Edith, because she couldn't tell him the truth. "Oh, James..." She stared at him now, the crushing realization coming upon her that her friend was standing there in workhouse stripes. He had a haunted look about him again, something she hadn't seen since he'd left his father's house. Like they'd been hurting him.

She clutched his hands. "Come on, James. You've seen now that they won't tell you about Donna. What good does it do to stay in the workhouse like this? You don't have to stay here – you can just leave. Leave and come with me. Please."

A shadow fell over James' face. He let go of her hands. "I told you, Edie," he said heavily. "I can't leave her."

"You don't even know..." Edith stopped before she could finish the hurtful sentence: ... *if she is alive or dead.* But he read it in her eyes, and it made him turn away.

"James, please!" Edith cried.

"Oi! You!"

The thundering voice came from a big man near the back door of the workhouse.

He had been smoking and talking with a companion; they both stood out in their ordinary clothes, so different from the ugly stripes. Now, though, he strode towards James, and he had a short whip in his hands. It had a sharp little lash, and James' body shuddered at the sight of it.

"James?" Edith quavered, terrified for him.

He glanced over his shoulder at her, such terror and desperation mingled in his face that she couldn't read the meaning in his eyes. Then he hurried back to his place, fell to his knees and started breaking up the stone as quickly as he could, his hands shaking where they clutched the hammer and chisel.

The man slapped the whip across his boot as he strode nearer. "What are you doing?" he demanded. "Who is she?"

James shot her another pleading look. "No one, sir."

This time, Edith understood. He wanted her to leave. He needed her to go away.

Everything inside her shattered, but she had no choice. She turned and left him.

Edith didn't even know why she'd come back to Covent Garden. It had been the sheer force of habit that had taken her back to her alleyway near the workhouse to sleep; she knew she should be looking for somewhere else to sleep, somewhere closer to Farringdon and her new patch on the edge of Whitechapel.

She had been hanging on to her alley for the sake of staying close to the workhouse, close to James.

But their encounter yesterday had made it very clear that James didn't want her.

The words sounded ludicrous even inside her own mind, but Edith knew they were true, and they pounded deeper and deeper into her soul with every step she took on throbbing feet.

She had eaten nothing yesterday, and barely slept. She felt like a ghost now, as though, at any moment, the pavement beneath her feet would realize that she was insubstantial, and that she would fall through it and just keep falling and falling right through the earth itself. As though she was too tired to thoroughly exist.

She blinked slowly as she plodded up to the gate of Covent Garden, almost asleep on her feet. She tried to lean into her exhaustion. It was less painful to be tired than to be this hungry.

Clutching her last shilling firmly in her palm, Edith tried to summon the energy to decide what she'd buy with that shilling. What would she be sure of selling?

She'd bought nearly half-a-crown's worth of flowers yesterday, and sold only a few: the rest had wilted, and she'd been forced to throw them away.

Now she had nothing left but this shilling, and she could only hope that she could make a little bit of money today, perhaps enough to eat as well as to buy stock for tomorrow.

She didn't know what to do if she couldn't sell anything today.

James would have known what to do. But James wasn't here now. And he didn't care.

Shoving her way through the crowds, Edith saw that some of the Christmas decorations around Covent Garden had been taken away.

As she watched, two workmen propped a tall ladder up against the nearest of the big buildings, and one of them laboriously climbed to the top to retrieve an enormous red-and-green wreath – decked out in red ribbons – at the top of a pillar. The sight of it turned Edith's stomach. Red ribbons. They were hateful things, absolutely hateful. She turned her face away.

She had reached Mr. Garrett's stall now, and she turned away from the sight of the Christmas decorations and instead towards the old man with his little stall. Instantly, her stomach swooped with dismay.

The old root-seller was here again with her wicker handcart and her pots, and she was happily loading them into her cart as though they didn't cost more money than Edith had ever made in a day: hothouse dahlias, tulips, and mignonettes, all blooming beautifully in their cheap pots.

There were a few sprigs of wallflowers lying on Mr. Garrett's table again, though. Edith hadn't been able to get any for days, and she knew that that was the reason why her flowers had been selling so poorly. Whitechapel people wanted wallflowers for whatever reason – and that was her only way to survive.

She wished she could rush up to him, push the malicious root-seller aside, and just grab the wallflowers for herself. But the root-seller was starting to pay Mr. Garrett, and maybe, if Edith stood very still, she would just forget about the cut flowers and go away.

For a few moments, Edith thought that her plan might just work. The root-seller grunted something to Mr. Garrett, then turned around and started pushing her handcart with the flowers on it.

Despite the fact that it was a very nice handcart, Edith noticed that the root-seller moved with difficulty, one hip swinging strangely as she waddled towards the crowd. She was heading through the people just past Edith, and Edith cringed, holding her breath in the desperate hope that the root-seller would simply pass her by.

She didn't. She stumped to a halt a few feet from Edith, panting and rubbing her hip, and then glanced over – looking Edith straight in the eye.

"You!" she barked, her eyes widening.

Edith backed away, her heart filling with hopeless terror. "Please, leave me alone," she cried. "Just go. I don't want any trouble. I just want to buy some cut wallflowers. You have all the roots you need."

She backed towards Mr. Garrett's table, clinging determinedly to her shilling. "I'll take them all, Mr. Garrett," she gasped, waving the shilling. "I will, I will. Please."

Mr. Garrett held up his hands, as if wanting to be left out of it.

The root-seller abandoned her cart and strode over to Edith, her eyes fixed upon her. "What's it to you, if you buy wallflowers or mignonettes instead?" she demanded, her voice very sharp.

"Please, ma'am, the people where I sell only want wallflowers. I think it's all they can afford." Edith swallowed her tears. "Please. I just need some flowers to sell. I'm hungry and alone and – and – "

"Stop that fuss at once," snapped the root-seller. "There's no need for tears, girl, and they won't get you anywhere in life either."

Edith swallowed them, mostly out of surprise. She stared at the root-seller with wide eyes.

"Come now." The root-seller grabbed Edith's arm in a fat-fingered little claw and dragged her over to Mr. Garrett. "Give the girl those wallflowers, Garrett."

Wordlessly, the old stallholder handed them over. Edith snatched them gratefully, not sure what was happening, but desperate to hold onto them. If the root-seller tried anything funny, she was quite sure that she could outrun her.

"What's your name, girl?" the root-seller demanded, watching as Edith shoved her shilling across the table to Mr. Garrett.

"Edith. Edith Atkinson."

"A silly-sounding name. Far too pretentious," sniffed the root-seller. "Are you good at selling flowers?"

"I... I think so," said Edith, trying to guess the right answer to the question.

The root-seller jerked her head in the direction of the handcart. "And you could push that cart, could you?"

"I... ah... yes?"

"Well then, what are you just standing about for?" The root-seller folded her arms. "Go on then – push it for me. It's not going to get to our spot all on its own."

Edith had no idea what was happening. She stared helplessly at the root-seller. "Excuse me, ma'am?"

The root-seller softened, a change so abrupt that she seemed for a few moments to be a completely different person.

"The truth is, girl, my old hip can't push that cart anymore," she said. "And you remind me of…" She stopped, then turned her face away. "I need someone to help me, and you could sell cut flowers with me. There's a space for you on the floor of my tenement."

Edith didn't know what to say. She didn't think she could say anything, even if she wanted to; she hardly knew whether she was terrified or relieved or overjoyed, but she was certainly overwhelmed.

"Where?" she managed at last.

"The tenement? Oh, it's in Seven Dials."

That was a long way from Whitechapel. What was more, it was even further from the workhouse. Edith didn't know if she could go back and see James if she went with this angry little root-seller, and she didn't know what the woman's intentions were. But the thought of being alone for the rest of the winter was too much for her.

Besides, James didn't want to see her. He had chosen the workhouse, after all.

"Please, ma'am," Edith said. "I would love to come with you."

"Well, don't be soppy about it," snapped the woman. "Push the cart. We'll miss the best hours of the morning at this rate."

"What – what do I call you?" Edith stammered.

"My name is Mercy Dawson, but none of that 'ma'am' or 'Mrs. Dawson' nonsense," said the root-seller indignantly. "You may call me Mercy. Now hurry up."

Edith seized the handles of the cart and pushed, and it was just as light and easy as she'd expected. She felt her heart lifting, too, just a little.

She had no idea what the future held for her now, but at least she wasn't completely alone in the present.

Chapter Nine

Two Years Later

1880

The sound of Mercy's voice certainly wasn't pleasant, but it carried far across the bustling streets of Soho as well-dressed gentlemen and flashy carriages rushed past. The pavement was comparatively empty here; most people had carriages, and seldom had to rely upon their own two feet. But the shops were all busy, with people hurrying in and out of them and to their cabs or carriages, and to those well-dressed folk, Mercy raised her cawing shout.

"London Pride! Candytufts!" she shouted. "Get your lovely balsam and lilies-of-the-valley! Stocks for your buttonhole! Marigolds for your garden! Violets for your study!"

Edith took a deep breath, holding up a rich sprig of moss roses. "Cut flowers! Cut flowers! Lovely cut flowers for your lady! Holly and mistletoe! Wreaths in all colours!"

Their cries were working, as usual. Mercy had been selling roots and potted flowers here for ten years, and these fashionable folk bought flowers by the dozen. They had just arrived on their corner, the bobby on the beat giving them a happy nod as he recognized them – so different from the policemen who had chased Edith from the various spots where she'd tried to sell flowers on her own.

Already, Edith spotted a familiar figure striding towards them: a fine, tall woman in a black-and-white uniform. Mrs. Alders was a housekeeper who bought flowers from them as many as three times a week.

"Mrs. Dawson!" she trilled, her eyes delighted as she hurried over to them. "I'm so glad to see you've been able to get some evergreens. Why, it just isn't Christmas without them!"

Every year, Edith thought that perhaps she would no longer hate the sound of the word *Christmas*. And every year, just like now, the word burned like a whip to her back. She forced a smile for Mrs. Alders' benefit. "We have wreaths too, with ribbons in all colours," she said. "They really brighten up a doorway."

"So you do!" Mrs. Alders ran a fingertip over the nearest wreath hanging from the front of Mercy's cart. It was wrapped in blue and red ribbon. "They're all lovely. I'll take four for the master's house, and a bit of mistletoe, and some of those sweet ditto that the mistress likes so much."

Edith started putting Mrs. Alders' purchases into a paper bag while Mercy counted out her change.

She shot a quick glance at the fistful of money that Mrs. Alders had just given her companion. They had just made more money in a single sale than they normally would in half a day.

Mrs. Alders hurried off, happily weighed down with her decorations, and Mercy gave Edith a flat-lipped approximation of a smile. "We'll eat well tonight, girl," she said. "I suppose there must be something to be said for all this Christmas nonsense."

"I don't like this time of year," Edith said. "Not one bit."

"It's all humbug if you ask me," grunted Mercy. "Spending a fortune on silly evergreens when you could have nice, colourful flowers lighting up your room! Why, they don't even stay green for all that long. And all the silly gifts and trees. It's just another excuse for the rich to fill their bellies and spend their money on stupid things, while the poor suffer."

Edith had heard the same rant many times before. She was aware that she and Mercy certainly benefited from the penchant of the rich – and the middle-class, for that matter – for buying "stupid things", but she was relieved that Mercy shared her hatred of Christmas.

It would be unbearable, she thought, to spend Christmas with someone who believed in all its frippery the way she had once.

It was difficult to believe that that girl in her memories had been Edith at all: that she'd sung Christmas carols and baked mince pies and gotten presents from Mama. She felt exhausted and angry thinking about it. How could she ever have hoped and trusted in that way? It was all foolishness. It had all betrayed her in the end.

"Stop that." Mercy cuffed her around the head, the sudden blow making Edith stumble. "Get that scowl off your face, girl. We can hate Christmas all we like, but our customers had better not know it."

Obediently, Edith lifted one of the wreaths out of the cart and held it up.

"Christmas! Christmas!" she shouted. "Evergreens for your Christmas decorations! Get your evergreens!"

~ ~ ~ ~ ~

The tenement wasn't much, but right now, its plainness was almost soothing. It had been a long day of hawking those wreaths and evergreens; they had all but sold out, and spent the whole afternoon twisting new wreaths for tomorrow. Edith's hands hurt as she pushed the door open and stepped into the tiny room, or, to be more accurate, their half of the room.

This was one of the older buildings in Seven Dials, and it felt as though it had once been destined for greatness; the rooms were large and spacious, with big windows that might have been pleasant if they had had glass panes in them.

Instead, the rooms had been cut in half by narrow wooden partitions that let through all the smells and sounds of the three drunken old men who lived in the other half. And the window was boarded up completely, with newspaper stuffed into the cracks where the drafts got in.

Still, having a home was a luxury that Edith wouldn't soon take for granted.

She pushed the handcart into its corner – Mercy insisted on having it carried up the flight of stairs to keep it from getting stolen – and shook out her tired, aching hands.

"There's no need to look so exhausted, girl," said Mercy, with unusual cheerfulness in her voice. The sales had been very good today. "There's hot chips and a bit of fish for supper, and there's no need to look so down in the mouth."

Edith knew that the main reason for Mercy's cheerfulness was the glass bottle in the little paper bag that she had tucked under her arm. She placed it on the small table that was wedged in one corner of the room, a trunk pushed under it; in the other corner was Mercy's narrow cot, with Edith's sleeping mat on the floor beside it.

The communal lavatory was down the hall. There was a rickety cupboard next to the bed, its door hanging on a single hinge, and a fireplace near the table. Edith pulled a bag of firewood from the handcart and went over to the fireplace.

By the time she had a fire going, Mercy had already eaten most of the fish. Edith contented herself with the chips and the scrap of fish that was left over.

She tried to enjoy it, knowing how foolish it was not to take full advantage of having a hot meal when the opportunity arose; things were easier now that she was with Mercy, but there were still many days when they could scrounge little other than some bread and vegetables. The good food still seemed to turn into flour in her mouth.

They had been putting up a Christmas tree near Mercy's corner today.

Every time Edith looked at it she remembered Donna's happy cry, Mama's body flying past her, and the sound of the wheels running over –

"Here," said Mercy, holding out the bottle. "You look like you need it."

Edith gave her an incredulous look. She'd tried a sip of Mercy's wine once, but it was vinegary stuff, and she didn't like it. "No, thank you. Enjoy it."

Mercy took another long swig. She'd already downed a quarter of the bottle; she was never generous before she'd had at least that much.

"We should have a toast," she said. "We made very good sales today."

Edith shrugged.

"Everyone is out there toasting hope and goodwill and peace and such nonsense." Mercy snorted, swigged from the bottle again. "Well, so far, we've made a bit of money off Christmas, at least. So here's to the stupidity of Christmas – long may it rot." She clinked the bottle against the cup of weak tea that Edith had in her hand.

"I hate Christmas," said Edith quietly.

"It's not fair. How rich folk get to spend all they like on silly parties and more food than they could ever eat, while some people are starving." Mercy shook her head. "Then they give a bit to charity just to feel better about themselves, and people are given oranges and beef in the workhouses, when they spend the rest of the year starving with no one to care."

Workhouse. Edith didn't even want to hear the word. Maybe she should have taken a bit of that wine, after all.

"That's not why I hate Christmas," she said.

Mercy knew. She was halfway down the bottle now, and starting to sway a little where she sat on her bed, but she fixed Edith with an alert and beady eye.

"Your mama was a fool to believe in it herself," she said bitterly.

"She was." Edith sighed. "But it was her only fault. And now she's gone."

"How long?" asked Mercy.

Edith was surprised by the answer. "Five years, this Christmas."

"Five years." Mercy shook her head, and took another long pull at the bottle. "For me, it's been nearly thirty."

Edith looked over at her, a little surprised. Maybe the old root-seller's wine was stronger than normal. Mercy never talked about her past.

"Nearly thirty?" she echoed.

"Yes. Twenty-eight this year." Mercy belched a little. "Since I lost my sister."

Edith stared at her. "Your sister?"

Mercy nodded. She stared down into the bottle for a few moments. "She was your age when she died. The most perfect, precious little doll of a thing.

Sweet as pie but had fire in her belly. Just like you. Same eyes, too. Same colour hair. It was like seeing a ghost, the first time we met at Covent Garden."

Edith didn't know what to say. For two years, she'd been wondering why grumpy old Mercy had ever asked her to join her, but perhaps now she could begin to understand.

"My mama was a lady of the night. Stupid woman – she led three of my other sisters into the same thing. Me too, for a little while." Mercy shrugged. "It was good money. But I couldn't let Emma fall into that life. I wouldn't. I kept her safe. I had someone teach her some letters. I had..." She stopped, and a lone tear trickled down her cheek. "I had hope for her. She loved Christmas, too. She'd bring me little gifts... trinkets. It was foolish." She wiped at the tear.

"You loved her very much," said Edith.

"More than life." Mercy looked up at her, and there was an unexpected vulnerability in the old woman's eyes. "But she drowned the winter she turned seventeen. A stupid, stupid accident. I had spent my whole life protecting her, and for nothing." She drank some more.

"I'm sorry."

"Why? You didn't kill her." Mercy gave a dark chuckle. "If you had, I would have torn your flesh from your bones. In any case, now I'm alone for Christmas. And so are you."

Edith said nothing. Now she understood, Edith thought, why there were never any Christmas decorations here.

Even the most rudimentary tenements in Seven Dials would attempt a little decoration, perhaps a candle or a sprig of holly on the door, but not here. This tenement was as plain and bare as any other day.

Christmas had become unbearable to them both.

"Twenty-eight years," mumbled Mercy. "Twenty-eight years alone. And for you, five years. That's a time, I suppose, when you're just a slip of a girl yourself."

"I haven't been alone for that long," said Edith. "There was someone else too... a... a friend."

Mercy leered at her. "A boy?"

"Perhaps." Edith felt her cheeks warming.

"Did he die, too?" asked Mercy heartlessly, drinking again.

"No... well..." With a shock of agony, Edith realized that she didn't know. "I don't think so. He went into the workhouse. I wouldn't."

"And it's just as well you didn't," said Mercy. "Dreadful places. Better to die on the streets."

"But I haven't seen him in two years." Edith's eyes filled with tears. "I miss him so terribly. I was a fool to leave him. I should have gone to see him more often."

"You were a fool." Mercy shook her head, her words slurring. "You're still a fool."

"Why?" Edith asked.

"Well, have you tried to find him?"

Edith's heart burned.

"No," she admitted.

Mercy sat up, wobbling a little, and fixed Edith with a rheumy, unfocused stare.

"Then you're worse than a fool; you're a coward, too. If you truly loved him, you should look for him before it's too late. You should let nothing stop you." She glared at Edith, tears running suddenly down her cheeks.

"Don't you know how lucky you are to have that option? Don't you know what I would do if I could find Emma somewhere? I would cross oceans. I would flatten mountains, I would – " She stopped, turning her face away, and then downed the rest of the bottle in a long gulp. "I would do anything," she muttered.

Again, Edith said nothing, her heart and mind too full to speak. In a few minutes, neither did Mercy; she was stretched out on her bed, snoring a boozy snore, the empty bottle lying on the floor beside the bed.

~ ~ ~ ~ ~

It took Edith more than two weeks to pluck up the courage to take Mercy's advice. Not that Mercy had nagged her about it: in fact, Edith doubted that Mercy even remembered their conversation when she woke up the next morning with a bad headache and a harsh tongue.

She knew that Mercy had been thoroughly drunk when she had said those words, when she had told Edith to go looking for James.

Yet the words wouldn't leave her. They had badgered her day and night as they hawked their evergreens, roots and cut flowers, and she couldn't forget them when she lay on her mat in the evenings and felt the pressure of the cold floor on her shoulders and thought of James.

She had been so heartbroken when she had left him, and she had promised herself she'd never go back to that workhouse, not after he told her to leave.

But years had soothed the fury of that pain, leaving behind a dull throb of longing and the growing conviction that Mercy was right. Edith was a coward and a fool not to go searching for him.

She felt foolish now, nonetheless, as she kept her arms wrapped around her body and walked down the pavement towards the workhouse in Mayfair. The scene was eerily similar to the last time she'd come to the workhouse: it was a Sunday morning, church bells tolling sonorously through the city, and she had to be back at the tenement by eleven o' clock so that she and Mercy could catch the Sunday crowd.

Christmas was less than a week away. Today, however, was anything but sunny. A sullen grey mist hung over the rooftops, turning them into gargoyles that leered and twisted in the corner of Edith's eye.

Her imagination was being fanciful, and she knew it. Still, she couldn't shake the nervousness that clung to her shoulders like a cobweb as she walked up to the workhouse. It had gotten bigger in the last two years, she realized; a new wing had been built on to its western side. Was that a good sign? She had no way of knowing.

The porter was different, at least. It was an older man this time, with a bushy white moustache and fingers that glowed red with cold. He was blowing on them as Edith approached, and raised equally bushy eyebrows when she said, "Excuse me, sir?" in her most polite voice.

"You're awful educated, for a ragamuffin," he said, but his tone was kind, and he gave her a gap-toothed leer. "Be a shame to see you end up in this place."

"I don't want to go into the workhouse, sir," said Edith quickly.

"Good, good. I'm glad to hear it." The old man tucked his fingers under his armpits. "What do you need then, young lady?"

Edith could hardly believe he was being helpful. "Actually, sir, I... I really need your help," she said eagerly, taking a step forward. "I'm looking for two friends of mine who went into the workhouse a couple of years ago. I just want to see them... to talk to them." Suddenly, her eyes were stinging with tears. "I miss them," she breathed.

"As well you might, young'un," said the porter with unexpected sympathy. "Well, try me. I've been here a year and a half, so I have, and I've made it my business to get to know everyone inside; someone must care for these poor sad souls, as the matrons don't, and neither do the supervisors, not one bit."

Edith's heart broke at the thought of Donna being surrounded by people who didn't care for her. Her young life had been so hard, but at least James had always been by her side – up until he'd taken her into the workhouse.

"Their name is Walsh," she said. "Donna and James Walsh." Her voice broke over their first names. It had been so long since she had said them, and they were so sweet on her tongue, yet the longing burned bitterly.

"Walsh, Walsh." The porter stroked his chin. "Did he go by Jim?"

"To his friends." Edith's heart leaped with hope, and she took an eager step forward, her hands clasped in front of her. "He's tall and skinny, with golden hair, and little Donna is a wisp of a thing with very big eyes, and..."

"I'm sorry, young lady." The porter's moustache drooped with genuine sorrow. "I can't help you. I don't know a Donna or a James Walsh... they must have moved on before my time."

"What?" Edith stepped back, reeling with horror.

"I'm truly sorry. If I knew them, I would tell you."

She didn't doubt the porter's words, but somehow it hadn't occurred to her that Donna and James might have moved on without her, that they might have abandoned her yet again — as she had abandoned them. Her heart thundered until it physically ached.

"But where did they go?" she breathed.

"I don't know. Perhaps somewhere better," said the porter encouragingly. "Maybe they found work somewhere. They could be just fine, you know."

Or they could be dead. The thought was intolerable, but so was the idea that maybe the porter was right.

Maybe James and Donna had found a better life, and they'd never come looking for Edith. They'd just left her behind in the past, like everyone did.

"Hodgkin!" shouted an angry voice from inside the workhouse. "What are you doing?"

The porter's eyes widened. "You'd better go, miss," he said. "The matron won't be happy if she sees you."

Edith turned and fled, tears pouring down her cheeks. She wished she'd never come.

She would rather be a coward than heartbroken.

Chapter Ten

Edith couldn't sleep that night despite the nagging exhaustion in her muscles and joints. She lay curled on her side on her sleeping mat, staring into the low flickering of the fire and listening to Mercy's deafening snores. In her first few weeks here, she'd found Mercy's snores irritating, struggling to stay awake with the sawing sound in her ears. Now, though, they were comforting.

They were evidence that she was not completely alone in the world; that someone else still existed who cared at least a little, just enough to give her somewhere to sleep and a little food.

With her head pillowed on her arm, Edith wondered if there was someone who was caring for James and Donna in this way. She wondered if they were still on this earth at all. Maybe the workhouse had claimed them, as it claimed so many victims. The thought of them buried in some pauper's grave was heart-wrenching.

Tears trickled down her cheeks, turning cold where the icy air touched them. She tried to find something in her heart to cheer herself, and her sleepy mind took her back to the last time she could remember being truly happy. Christmas Eve, with Mama, James, and Donna. They hadn't had all that much – sausages and potatoes instead of roast chicken that Christmas Eve – but her heart had never been so full. She remembered their laughter as they played charades, their joy as they sang Christmas carols together…

Her heart smote her. She thought of what Mama had always said about her future, how bright it was. Mama had had so much hope and so much faith.

And it had all been false.

Why had Mama allowed her to believe that there was good in the world, that there was hope in Christmas? There was none. She was gone. James was gone. Donna was gone.

She pulled her blanket over her head and cried herself to sleep.

~ ~ ~ ~ ~

"Brighten your doorways!" Edith swung the hateful wreath in the air over her head. "Brings cheer to the heart! Perfect for decorating your dining room! Wreaths! Beautiful Christmas wreaths!"

"All right, child," said Mercy grumpily. "That's enough of that."

Edith lowered her wreaths. "But we've only sold two."

"Yes, but anyone can see your bitterness from a mile away," Mercy grunted. "We only have three days left before Christmas – we need to sell these things while we have the chance. Now give me those. You hawk the flowers."

Relieved, Edith pushed the wreaths into Mercy's hands. They had red ribbons on them, the disgusting things, and she couldn't get far enough away from them.

"Look at that old biddy." Mercy gave a little chuckle; it sounded false and strange. "Her little dogs are causing her plenty of trouble."

Edith looked up, a little surprised. She hadn't known that Mercy had a sense of humour at all. She was gesturing towards a very tall, very thin elderly woman who was drifting down the street, insubstantial as a will o' the wisp, her pale blue clothes streaming behind her as three little fluffy dogs practically dragged her in all directions.

They were approaching a lamppost, and the lady and her dogs met their inevitable doom when they all went in different directions around the post, necessitating a lot of tittering from the lady and disentangling of leads.

Edith supposed it was an entertaining scene, but she turned away, picking up some roots. "Marigolds, heliotropes!" she called without enthusiasm. "Nice roots!"

Mercy shot Edith a quick glance. "I think we'll have a little extra money again tonight, if we do as well as we've been doing lately," she said. "You can choose what we have for supper."

Edith gazed at Mercy vaguely, and it occurred to her that perhaps the old lady was trying to cheer her up.

Mercy had never made an offer like that before. There was a hint of desperation in her eyes, but something else, too, something that she only sometimes saw there, usually when Mercy didn't know she was looking: compassion.

She knew she should make an effort, for Mercy's sake. "Thank you. That would be nice."

"Good!" said Mercy. "Now sell those flowers." She held up the wreaths and started calling in her distinctive, croaking voice. "Wreaths! Christmas wreaths!"

Edith summoned up some energy, holding up a potted musk-plant. "Musk and mignonette! Michaelmas daisies! Hothouse china-asters! Best prices in Soho!"

No one even looked her way, and she lowered the roots with a sigh. She just didn't have the strength for this. She didn't have the strength for anything. Christmas couldn't be over soon enough; perhaps then she would forget about James and Donna and the future she'd dreamed of, and accept her unhappy lot at last.

"What are you doing?" Mercy wheeled to face her, exasperated. "You need to sell those flowers, girl."

"No one is interested," said Edith shortly.

"People aren't interested because you're not trying."

"I *am* trying."

"Well, you have the appeal of a dead fish, girl. Try harder!"

Mercy's grating tone sliced through Edith's mind with physical pain. She was just so tired. Gritting her teeth, she hissed, "I can't. Stop shouting at me."

Mercy's eyes widened at this display of insolence, which shocked even Edith; she didn't think she'd ever talked back to Mercy, or to anyone, in this way before. Mercy took an angry step towards her, her eyes blazing. "What was that?"

Edith wanted to cower, but something bitter and horrible was rising up inside her, and she didn't want to resist. She leaned into it; it was easier to feel angry than to feel scared and abandoned and grieving.

"I said, stop shouting at me!" she snapped back, her voice rising. "I'm doing my best! Can't you see that?"

Mercy gasped at Edith's tone. Drawing back a hand, she dealt Edith a mighty slap to the back of the head. It barely hurt, but its impact rang through her mind, fuelling her bitter rage. Stumbling back a step, Edith stared at her.

"Don't you dare use that tone with me ever again, you young hussy," spat Mercy. "Do I make myself clear?"

Edith wanted to shout, but across the street, a familiar figure caught her eye. It was Mrs. Alders, come like clockwork to buy flowers. She was hesitating, however, looking at Edith and Mercy with wide eyes.

"Yes," Edith muttered, dropping her eyes. She didn't want to miss out on a sale.

Mercy followed her gaze, cursing under her breath. "Now you've done it," she muttered. "She won't come here now." She raised one of the wreaths, nonetheless. "Mrs. Alders! Another pretty wreath for you today?"

But Mrs. Alders had already turned and hurried off into the traffic.

A wave of helpless frustration, guilt, and anger washed over Edith. She knew that shouting at Mercy was irrational and would only cause problems for them both. Yet when she wanted to apologize, the words wouldn't come out.

She grabbed her handful of cut flowers again instead and started hawking them hopelessly to the heartless crowds of people who rushed past, stone-faced beneath the wreaths hanging from every lamp-post and through the golden candlelight shining from every window and beneath the bright bunting strung from rooftop to rooftop.

Cheer, goodwill, generosity – the decorations were screaming these things from every corner, yet none of them seemed to have pierced the hearts of the people that Edith saw now. Or her own heart, either.

~ ~ ~ ~ ~

Christmas Eve came, which was both a dread and a relief for Edith as she pushed the handcart back towards their tenement through the half-finished, half-forgotten streets of Seven Dials. She had been dreading Christmas Day for weeks, but at least, by tomorrow afternoon, it would all be over.

In just a few days all these hateful decorations would be gone, and she was almost finished with hearing the greeting she hated the most.

A young woman was crossing the street in front of her, hardship written in the patches and rips on her faded clothing, three little children clinging to her skirts.

She was carrying a pail that had a leak in it; one of the children was trying in vain to keep a finger over the hole as water trickled out onto the street.

Every drop of that water had been pumped by hand from the pump across the road. The children had wide, hollow eyes; one stumbled along on bandy legs, his bones twisted by malnourishment.

The woman, Edith could see, was pregnant again, yet her own arms were little more than skin-wrapped bone. Edith wondered if the child in her womb would live to take a single breath. There was a black bruise across her cheek, loud and ugly against the softness of her skin.

Edith didn't realize that she was staring until the woman glanced down at one of the children, and their eyes met unexpectedly. Edith lowered her eyes, embarrassed, but somehow a smile tugged at the woman's lips.

"Merry Christmas!" she said.

Edith felt something break inside her. She wanted to scream at this woman. "Look around you!" she wanted to cry. "What could be merry in your life? Why are you spouting this nonsense?" But she kept her mouth shut and went on pushing the cart instead, her muscles toiling as it bumped through slush-filled holes. The snow was pretty on the cobbled streets of the better-off parts of London; here, it was an inconvenience, a hazard, and a smelly, yellow-grey eyesore.

Yet among the holey roads, and the boarded-up windows and cracked plaster and peeling paint and missing doors, there were Christmas decorations even here. Little sprigs of dry holly hanging over doorways.

Stubs of candles in the windows. Scraps of old ribbon tied around posts and bent, malnourished trees. Pathetic attempts at injecting a little hope and light into the dreariness of Seven Dials.

Edith was relieved when they finally made it back into their own tenement, where there was nothing; just the bare walls, the floor, the bed and mat like it was at any other time of the year. Mercy slammed the door shut behind them, shuddering a little. "Ugh – there's a nasty cold wind outside."

It hadn't seemed colder than normal to Edith, so she just shrugged and took a newspaper-wrapped parcel out of the handcart. It had been another day of poor sales. There would be no hot fish or coffee tonight; she'd scrounged two carrots and a wrinkled beet to make into soup. Along with a loaf of yesterday's bread, it would have to do for a Christmas Eve supper. She placed the parcel on the table, unwrapped it, and started cutting the vegetables.

Mercy sat down on the edge of her bed, as usual. She studied Edith for a few long moments, and Edith braced herself, knowing that she was about to get another tongue-lashing. Mercy was blaming her for the poor sales.

Edith supposed that she did have a hand in them; after all, rich folk didn't want to buy their evergreens from a girl obviously lacking in the foolishness of "Christmas cheer".

"Edith." Mercy stopped.

Edith turned, surprised. Mercy almost never called her by her actual name. Dread curled in her stomach, and she stared at her speechlessly for a few moments, her heart pounding.

Was Mercy about to tell her to leave? If she did, what would Edith do? She had nowhere to go. She would be all alone.

Mercy seemed to be wrestling with some inner struggle. Her mouth worked, her eyes narrowing as emotion filled them. Edith thought it was anger, but then suddenly, tears appeared in them, deep and shimmering.

"Mercy?" she stammered out.

Mercy let out a terrible oath that raised the hairs on the back of Edith's neck, then stood up, folding her arms. "Something has to change," she said, her tone sharp and gruff despite the tears in her eyes.

"Wh-what do you mean?" Edith's stomach clenched. Was she about to become homeless again?

"You can't survive like this!" Mercy burst out suddenly. A tear escaped, running down her cheek, and she stomped across the room and seized Edith roughly by her upper arms. "You can't go on like this, and I can't watch you go on like this, either!"

Shocked by the outburst, Edith was silent. Words poured from Mercy like water from a flooded river.

"You have to get your head on straight again, girl!" Mercy barked, a sob hiding in her voice now. "If you keep on sinking like this, you'll never stop — you'll just sink and sink and sink deeper into a black pit until you can see no way out. Until you get to a place where you can no longer remember what hope felt like. Where you couldn't hope anymore even if you tried!"

"What is there to hope for?" Edith mumbled.

"I don't know, but there has to be something." Mercy's grip tightened on Edith's arms. "If not for me, then there will be something for *you*. There has to be. Because if this world doesn't hold any goodness, any love, any grace, any joy, any hope for a girl like you – a perfect, brave, sweet, loving little girl like you – " Abruptly, Mercy dropped her hands to her sides, turning away. "Then nothing is right with this world at all."

Edith stared at her. The emotion she had seen in Mercy's eyes and felt in her grip shocked her, because it was love: deep and powerful love, something akin to what she'd felt in Mama.

"Mercy," she whispered.

Mercy turned back to her, tears still glittering on her cheeks. "You have to find hope again, Edith," she said. "Or you'll forget how, and you'll become a grumpy old woman with nothing left in the world. I never had my miracle, but there has to be a Christmas miracle in the world for you – oh, there must be, there must! But that's the thing about miracles.

I never believed I would have mine, and it never came. Maybe, if you believe in yours, then you will be given it. I don't know. But I do know you can't go on like this." She grabbed Edith's hands again. "I can't bear for you to go on like this."

"I don't know..." Edith's voice broke. She hadn't felt like crying, but suddenly she was sobbing, tears cascading down her cheeks. "I don't know – how to – hope again." The words came out brokenly, half swallowed by the sobs.

"You have to start by not giving up." Mercy squeezed her hands. "I don't know what it is that you're hoping for, or what you went looking for the other day when you came back so disheartened, but you can't give up on it.

You have to go after it again somehow, Edith. I don't know how. But you can't give up. You can't. You're too young... life has to have something to offer you."

Edith thought of what the porter had said. James and Donna weren't in the workhouse, and hadn't been, for months. But maybe they were still alive out there somewhere; maybe there was still a chance that Edith could find them, if she didn't give up.

Something flickered in her chest. It was very small, but it was something, and it had to be hope. She looked into Mercy's desperate eyes and realized that Christmas had brought her one good thing, after all – it had brought her Mercy.

Her sobs flowed anew. And for the first time, Mercy put her arms around her and held her very tightly.

Chapter Eleven

Edith could hear a Christmas carol filtering into the still, wintry air from the windows of the church on the street corner. It was a big church, splendidly Gothic with snow dusted along the strong edges of its buttresses and parapets, and the sternness of it had been softened by the Christmas decorations that were hanging all over its facade.

"O holy night, the stars are brightly shining…"

The soaring tones of the congregation's voices, and the booming note of the organ, must have been beautiful to some. But Edith could only remember the carollers that had sung this very same carol on the day that Mama died. She clutched her coat a little more tightly around her shoulders, as though that could keep out both the sound and the memory, and hurried down the street as quickly as her feet could carry her.

The morning was bitterly cold. It wasn't snowing, but the sky was low and heavy. Not a breath of wind stirred last night's snow where it lay thickly on the pavement, her feet crunching on it as she made her way towards the workhouse.

Edith's breaths came quickly, curling around her face as steam, and not just because of how briskly she was walking. Nervousness thrilled through every fibber of her body, a hot current that made it difficult to concentrate on where she was going. Last night, she had somehow begun to believe that maybe she would be able to find James and Donna again.

But what if she didn't?

The question hung on her shoulders like a burden as she walked up to the front of the workhouse. A pitiful wreath made a sad attempt at livening its cold and austere facade. There was no one at the door, and Edith stumbled up to it, shivering in the cold. She could hear voices from inside the workhouse. They sounded like they were singing.

Maybe it hadn't been a good idea to come here on Christmas Day. But Edith knew that she would never have had the courage to do it if she'd waited a moment longer. Taking a deep breath, she raised a fist and hammered on the door.

A cold stretch of silence passed. Edith wrapped her arms around herself against the frigid air. Surely someone had to be close enough to hear her? She knocked again, harder, this time, and the door finally swung open to reveal a tall woman with a wide, angry mouth that was pulled down at the corners.

Her eyes flashed up and down Edith, and then she stepped back, holding the door open. "Second door on the left," she droned. "Strip your clothes. Personal items will be retained for safekeeping."

"Excuse me?" said Edith.

"Well, do you want to come into the workhouse or not?" barked the woman.

"Not! I mean – I don't, thank you," Edith stammered.

"Then why are you here?" the woman demanded.

"Because I – I need to find out about a friend of mine, who was... who might be in here," said Edith.

The woman glared at her. "You're coming to me with this on Christmas Day?"

"Please, ma'am." Edith stepped forward, fearful that she might slam the door on her. "Please, I just want to know if he lives or dies. I haven't seen or heard from him in so long, and I miss him so much, and I just need to know what happened to him."

"Go away."

Edith stood firm, remembering Mercy's words about not giving up. They lent her strength now. "Ma'am, please, I won't go. I need to hear what happened to my friends. I'll sleep on your threshold if I have to; I'll hammer on this door night and day, I'll..."

The woman sighed. "I'll look in my ledger," she snapped, "but then you have to leave at once."

"Oh, yes, thank you, ma'am!" Edith gasped, surprised and delighted. "I will, I will, I just – "

"Stop that noise and wait here. I'm getting my ledger."

The woman slammed the door deafeningly in Edith's face, and for a few horrible moments Edith thought that the woman had left her out there.

She was about to make good on her promise and start hammering on the door again when it swung open, revealing the woman with a large, leather-bound book in her arms.

"Name?" she demanded.

"James and Donna Walsh. They were siblings."

The woman thumbed through the ledger, running her finger down a line of *W*s. "No," she said, snapping the book shut. "I don't have any Walshes here. Does that satisfy you?"

"But please, ma'am, I know they were here. Can you tell me what happened to them?"

"No. This ledger is all I have. I've been here for three months, and the previous woman – well!" She snorted, raising her chin. "She kept no records to speak of, none at all."

Edith's heart sank. "So you don't know what happened to them?"

"Nobody does." The woman stepped back. "Good day to you. And merry Christmas."

The words were flat and cold. She slammed the door in Edith's face.

~ ~ ~ ~ ~

It was late in the afternoon by the time Edith finally made her way back to Seven Dials. The streets were absolutely empty except for a few homeless people, slumped hopelessly on corners; for them, as for Edith, Christmas was just another day.

She struggled to keep her spirits from failing her as she dragged herself through the bleak and empty streets.

A cold wind had risen from the north, blowing directly in her face as she struggled up the street. Mercy had said not to give up. But where could Edith go now to find James and Donna? If the workhouse didn't know where they'd gone, who did?

She fought to keep the questions at bay, clinging to some semblance of hope. She'd tell Mercy what had happened when she got back to the tenement.

The old lady had still been asleep when Edith had left, and Edith hadn't wanted to disturb her. Now she could tell her anything, and maybe Mercy would know what to do.

"It's me!" she called out, climbing the stairs to their tenement. The stale, beery smell from the tenement beside theirs was thicker than ever as Edith pushed the door open; the old men had been celebrating, she supposed.

She wrinkled her nose, stepping into the tenement and closing the door. "Oh, Mercy, you won't believe what happened. The matron of the..."

She stopped. She'd expected to see Mercy sitting on her bed, staring into the fire like she usually did. Instead, the fire had gone out. The hearth was cold and grey, the room twilit. A chill ran through Edith, and there was more to it than just the temperature of the air.

The covers on Mercy's bed were still rumpled, and there was a shape underneath them. A motionless shape.

"Mercy?" Edith croaked.

There was no reply. No movement.

Just silence.

Edith's heart had frozen in her chest. It felt as though the walls were collapsing in on her, as though the world was suddenly too small to contain her. She took a few steps forward on weak, wobbling legs, aware that she was shaking from head to foot.

"Mercy?" she whispered.

Her outstretched hand found the edge of the blanket and pulled, and her scream stuck in her throat, frozen with terror.

Mercy lay peacefully on her side, her knees drawn up in front of her, her head pillowed on her hands. Her hair was a plume around her head, soft and grey as smoke. Her eyes were closed.

She looked like she was sleeping, except that her face was the colour of the dirty snow outside. And no matter how hard Edith stared, she couldn't see any movement in her chest, any stirring of breath around her nose.

No matter how loudly she screamed, Mercy didn't stir. No matter how much she shook her, the old lady didn't wake up.

In the early hours of Christmas morning, Mercy Dawson had died quietly in her sleep.

~ ~ ~ ~ ~

Edith had had to sell the handcart to have Mercy buried in a pauper's grave.

The man who had come to take Mercy away had told Edith that she wouldn't want to go to the cemetery and see her buried.

But it felt so wrong to let them just take her away like that, not even in a cotton, just wrapped in some old burlap. Edith was allowed to sit quietly in the back of the wagon, just behind the heaps of dead people that the two men had collected through the day.

They smelled. Some of them had awful stains on the burlap that was wrapped around them. Despite the fact that they were all wrapped up like that, Edith had no difficulty knowing which one was Mercy.

Grief had become her shadow, yet she was still surprised with its keen painfulness as she tried to imagine her future without Mercy.

There would be no coming home to the tenement, no buying roots from Mr. Garrett in Covent Garden. This she knew: she had spent everything she had just to have Mercy buried. There was only enough money left to buy some cut flowers

When they came to the cemetery, Edith was told to stand to one side, and the men approached a gigantic hole in the earth that smelled like death. Little heaps of straw were lying around it, and one of the men set them alight, filling the scene with a dense and acrid smoke that smelled only a little better than the reek rising from within the hole.

When Edith looked more closely through the veil of smoke, she saw little heaps in the hole – people. People who had not so much been buried in that hole as that they had simply had some soil hastily shovelled over them.

Horror clutched at her stomach. There would be no headstone for Mercy. She wouldn't even have a grave her of her own.

She was going to be buried in here with hundreds of strangers, like the unwanted bones of cattle thrown into a pit and forgotten when they were no longer useful to society.

She stepped forward, wanting to stop the men and beg her for her own grave, but they were already carrying Mercy's body into the grave. They dropped her on the ground beside one of the half-buried ones.

There was a terrible thump as the body hit the ground, and Edith imagined Mercy's limbs jumping and flopping, her head thudding against the earth. It was too much even to think of, let alone to witness, and Edith wanted to flee.

But she didn't. She stayed and watched as one by one, the bodies were dumped onto the dirt. There was no reverence for them; the men were working quickly, aware that the day was slipping past.

They tossed them down like they were sacks of flour, the way they had dropped Mercy as though she was nothing but an inanimate object, instead of the one person who had been holding Edith's world together for the past years.

Then again, Edith realized with a terrible shock as the men started to shovel earth over the bodies, that thing in the burlap wrapping *was* an inanimate object. Mercy herself – the Mercy with the sharp tongue and angry fist and good heart – was gone.

She had left this world behind for another, and now there was nothing left of her, just a thing in a sack that was being buried like rubbish.

That was when Edith could no longer stand it.

She turned and hurried out of the cemetery and into the snowy night, tears streaming down her cheeks in the frigid air. The crunch of the snow under her feet sounded like the crumpling of her world.

∼ ∼ ∼ ∼ ∼

Edith didn't return to the tenement. She wasn't sure that she would easily be able to find it, in any case; she had not been paying attention when they bumped and rattled their way across the city to the cemetery where Mercy was buried.

Even if she could, what good would it do? Tomorrow was Monday, and the landlord would be around asking for money that Edith just didn't have. She would have been evicted then, in any case.

Instead, even though she hadn't eaten all day, Edith wanted nothing more than to go to sleep. It was a cold, bleak evening, with snow driven on the teeth of the wind, the sky utterly black behind the feeble attempts of streetlamps to illuminate a little of the night.

Edith stumbled down the street, not knowing where she was going. It was a middling sort of district, one that looked vaguely familiar, but through her fog of grief and loneliness, Edith struggled to recognize any of it.

It was only when she stumbled right into the market square that Edith realized her feet had carried her to Farringdon Market. She had been here a few times to buy flowers and roots when Mr. Garrett had been ill; it was far less fashionable than Covent Garden, but at least she would be able to get some flowers here tomorrow morning.

Hopefully she would be able to hawk her flowers on her old patch along the edge of Whitechapel.

Of course, Finsbury would be closer. But that was where...

No. Not tonight. Edith shook her head, as if to physically dislodge the thought. She wasn't going to think about Mama tonight, or about the house right on the edge between Finsbury and Barbican where she had been so happy so long ago.

Instead, she had to find somewhere to sleep until the market opened and she could buy those flowers. There was a park somewhere close by, wasn't there? It was hard to think; her thoughts seemed to move slowly, as though fighting through deep mud, the bog of her grief.

Edith thought it had been slightly to the west. She started walking, the cold wind slicing through her clothing. Maybe she could huddle underneath a hedge for the night, if she could find a park.

It wasn't a park, however. When Edith reached it, she recognized it at once: an open space clad in greyish, polluted snow, surrounded by a low wall, with bare-limbed trees standing around the edges.

There were no open spaces or ponds here, though. Just headstones. Row upon row of headstones, extending into the night.

It was a cemetery. Edith backed away, terrified by the taint of death, but her eye caught a nearby bench in front of one of the fancier headstones.

Someone had put it there for the grieving to sit upon, and it was nicely sheltered by a hedge and a bush of holly.

She hated the sight of the holly with its absurd red berries, and the sight of the headstones with their sombre silhouettes, but the space underneath the bench was sheltered and dry, and her bones were so weary and so cold.

She had nowhere else to go. Slowly and stiffly, she pulled herself up and over the wall; the gates were locked, but the wall was easily scaled.

Then she shuffled through the snow, trying not to walk over any graves, and curled up beneath the bench on the dirt. She had brought her few belongings with her, including the blanket from her sleeping mat; and the thin cover left behind on Mercy's bed.

She had thought that she would lie awake, but her exhaustion was absolute. It wasn't long before she sank into an uncomfortable sleep.

~ ~ ~ ~ ~

The sound of weeping echoed through the air. It was a thin, wailing sound, rising and falling in a continuous moan of absolute suffering, and it dragged Edith from the clutches of her sleep. She blinked in sudden brightness, confused for a moment, wondering why Mercy had turned on the lights; it was Edith's task to make the morning tea and get Mercy out of bed every morning.

Then she remembered that Mercy was dead, and that she was sleeping under a bench in the cemetery, and that the sun must have risen while she was asleep. And someone was crying in that terrible, constant wail, someone close by.

Edith wanted to go back to sleep. Her body seemed ready to simply switch off, and descend quietly into the blackness where she knew neither pain nor fear nor hunger. She closed her eyes, but the darkness that met her was so absolute that it frightened her, and she forced herself to move.

Pain lanced through her hands and feet; they had grown so cold. And hunger clutched at her belly, clawing at her from the inside like a rabid animal.

The weeping continued outside, piercing her mind. She wished it would stop. Peering out from under the bench, she blinked against the sunshine.

The crying was coming from beside one of the nearby graves. A thin woman was standing in front of the headstone, covering her face with her hands and crying. A young man who could have been her double had an arm around her, but Edith could see the glimmer of tears on his cheeks, and the slight shudder of his shoulders as he held back his own tears.

The woman paused in her crying to give a hiccuping sob, and Edith hoped she would stop. Instead, she cried out, "Oh, Rupert, Rupert!" and began to cry again.

"Now, now," mumbled the man, but his own voice was wispy and broken.

"Another Christmas without him!" sobbed the woman. "How can it be, brother? It's been three years, and yet every time the door opens, I still hope that – that he would – "

"I know," murmured the man. "I know."

"There is so much I wanted to say to him. So much that I… that…" The woman's words were swallowed by weeping.

Edith closed her eyes. She should get up and go to Farringdon Market, and buy some flowers and find somewhere to sell them. But how? She couldn't go back to Soho; it was too far away, and besides, the people there wanted roots more than cut flowers, and she didn't have any. It would only be a matter of days before some other root-seller moved in there.

She had nowhere to sell flowers. What was the use? Edith was about to close her eyes again when the woman spoke.

"Oh, Rupert, I wish... I wish I could go shopping for ridiculous Christmas gifts for you one more time." A laugh entered her voice, broken by grief. "Do you remember, Johnny?"

"Of course. Rupert was impossible when it came to gifts. One could never get him a cigar case or a wristwatch. He hated such trinkets."

"Remember the year that I bought him boots, out of desperation?" The woman tried to laugh again, but sobbed instead. "He only wanted useful things."

"Except for flowers," said the man. "He loved flowers."

"So he did! He always had them in his study while he was painting... oh... oh, Johnny." The woman's voice shattered. "I should have brought flowers."

"Where would we have gotten them?" sighed the man, hugging her a little more tightly. "There aren't any flower-sellers at the gate here anymore."

Edith's eyes widened. That was something she could do: sell cut flowers at the gate to the grieving. The thought made her heart falter for a moment. How could she deal with that? With seeing one grieving family after another pass by her?

But the thought was irrelevant. Her heart would break, but it would still be beating. It was a way for her to survive.

She waited for the grieving woman to leave with her brother, then crawled out from under the bench and stuffed her blanket back into her bag. Hoisting it onto her shoulder, she plodded out into the street, aware that she was covered in dirt. Farringdon Market was just a few blocks from here, but it seemed a terribly long way away. Instead of looking up at the distance, she looked down at her feet, and watched them move her forward, one step at a time.

She only had the courage for the very next step. Nothing more.

Chapter Twelve

One Year Later

1881

It seemed as though a thousand years had passed since Mercy's death, and yet Christmas was only just approaching.

Edith stood at the gate to a small cemetery on the edge of Barbican, praying that someone in the crowd shuffling past her would come inside. There were only a handful of graves here, but there was an old man who visited his wife's grave almost every day and could be counted upon to buy a little bunch of flowers for it, even though he himself barely seemed to have any clothes to wear. He hadn't come for two days now, and Edith was growing desperate. There were few others who came to this tiny cemetery next to a run-down little church huddling down between the warehouses that had risen up around it in recent years. It seemed mostly forgotten, and Edith herself felt invisible.

The street itself was busy. It was just after ten in the evening, and people were hurrying back to their tenements in Whitechapel from the many warehouses and factories in Barbican. These were hollow-eyed, pale-faced people dressed in rags, their bodies disfigured by endless work, their breaths rasping audibly as they came past.

Many were coughing and spluttering as they walked, allowing saliva to drip down their lower lips and chins as though wiping it away was more effort than they had left in them for this day. Most of them were children. Edith wondered if any of them had ever learned their letters. If there was a dame school here somewhere for them.

She knew she shouldn't think about dame schools now, or ever. It was hard not to think of Mama, however. The owner of the warehouse across the street had, absurdly, decided to decorate the warehouse for Christmas. There were wreaths on the doors, all covered in holly and ribbons; she had overheard the workmen talking about the price that the owner had paid for those wreaths, and wondered if she shouldn't start making some.

No. Her hand tightened on the four bunches of cut flowers she was holding; all she had been able to buy for today. She wasn't touching evergreens. She was going to pretend that Christmas didn't exist.

Maybe then it would pass her by, and she wouldn't feel the icy touch of its many tragedies.

All Christmas meant to her this year was an added layer of grief, and the knowledge that she would be struggling to make money.

People just didn't come to visit graves at Christmastime; they were too busy celebrating with the living to make time for the dead. Edith had begun to feel like she was dead herself. She spent more time with the graves than with living people, and her heart felt like the frozen earth – hard and empty.

She was just starting to think that she would make no sales at all today when two young men turned away from the crowd and started moving purposefully towards her. They were scruffy men, one with long, greasy black hair, the other with a few straggles of reddish beard. As they headed towards her, Edith felt an uncomfortable little shiver run up her spine.

She brushed it aside, holding up her flowers with renewed purpose. At least she didn't have to cry her wares at the gate of the cemetery; instead, as the men approached, she spoke in quiet, reverent tones.

"Come to pay your respects, good sirs?" she said. "Care for a flower to put on the grave?"

"Oh, I'd like a flower, all right," said the bearded one. His eyes travelled up and down her body.

"I have violets for you, lovely and fresh," said Edith. "Or perhaps your loved one enjoyed roses more? They're real beauties, straight from the hothouse." She held them out.

"I'd say it's more of a marigold I'm looking for," leered the long-haired one. "Pretty and bright and young."

He reached out, touching the back of a grubby finger to Edith's cheek, and suddenly her heart was hammering out of her chest. She pulled back, forcing a quick, smooth smile.

"I beg your pardon, gentlemen," she said. "I'm not that kind of flower-seller." As she'd grown older, she'd become more and more aware of the girls who flaunted their bodies as part of their wares. Despite her conservative rags, many men still took their chances.

"Come now," said the bearded one. "You're pretty enough to be one."

"That's as may be, sir, but I'm not." Edith backed away towards the cemetery, shooting a quick glance to the back gate. If she moved fast, she could dart between the graves and escape.

"Well, it's never too late to change, is it?" The long-haired one plunged a filthy hand into his pocket and pulled out half-a-crown. "Come on then. Give it a try."

Half-a-crown. It was more money than Edith made even on a good day, but the thought of what he wanted and the expression in his eyes made her stomach turn. She took another step backwards, reaching out her free hand to rest it on the gate latch. "No thank you, sir."

Something changed in the long-haired one's eyes. Hunger turned sinister, and he was suddenly up against her, one hand closing on her arm, the other searching the front of her dress, prying, squeezing. "I offered to pay you," he hissed, his breath foul on her face. "Remember that."

Edith's fingers closed on the gate latch, and she wrenched it open, stumbling backwards through it. The man's hand tightened on her arm and for a terrible instant Edith thought they would go over backwards with him on top, and that would be the end for her.

But somehow she kept her feet; she heard the crunch of her flowers against his chest and knew they were ruined, but there was no time for despair. Flailing wildly, her free hand caught his face, found his eye, dug a finger into it. She had learned not to fight fair. He let out a terrible wail and collapsed backwards, and that was all the room Edith needed.

She was off, flying through the cemetery in the darkness, knowing her way easily among the gravestones. They were shouting in pursuit, but they didn't know where to run; she heard thuds and oaths as they crashed into the headstones. Arms flying, eyes focused,

Edith fled, skirting around the back of the church where a large bush stood in the corner. She threw herself to the ground and scrambled under it, coming to a breathless halt in the shadow of the bush just as the running feet started to catch up to her.

Lying under the bush, holding her breath despite the fire in her lungs, Edith listened to their voices. She listened to the names that they called her, to the curses and the slurs. Somehow, she kept absolutely quiet until their footsteps receded off down the street again. It was only then that she allowed herself to weep.

She had realized that it was a holly bush she was cowering under. Christmas and all its misfortunes, it seemed, would not let her escape.

~ ~ ~ ~ ~

The next day dawned as bleak and foggy as Edith's mind. She had eaten nothing the day before, and little more than a bit of fish and vegetable soup the day before that, and now she was having trouble convincing herself to rise from the spot where she slept.

It was in a little nook against the wall of the church, with a sack pulled over her body for a blanket. The church's caretaker would arrive in a few minutes, and if he discovered her, he might chase her off.

What would that matter? Edith felt numbly through her pockets one more time, but there was nothing in them. Even her cold and aching fingers would have been able to find a coin. But there was nothing.

All she had had left were those expensive hothouse flowers she'd been trying to sell yesterday. And when she had gone back last night to look for them, when the men had safely gone, she'd found them hopelessly crushed and trampled into the snow.

There were no flowers left, and besides, Edith was beginning to realize that no one would have bought them even if she had managed to hold onto them.

If even the old widower wasn't coming to the cemetery at this time of year... well, then this cemetery had turned out to be yet another dead end.

Tears stung her eyes, and she squeezed them shut.

Edith had been bouncing from one cemetery to the other ever since Mercy had died.

Sometimes the caretakers would chase her off, or some root-seller would shoulder in on her patch and drive her away, and sometimes, like now, the business would simply peter out until it was worthless to keep trying.

She doubted she had been able to stay with any cemetery for longer than a month, some of them, much less.

And she could think of nowhere else to go now. Nowhere except…

No. Again, Edith stopped her thoughts. She wasn't going to go back to the cemetery where Mama was buried.

It just held far too many memories, and besides, what could she expect to see there? A cracked headstone, an overgrown and neglected grave? No one had been to Mama's grave since she and James and Donna had had to move out of the house all those years ago.

Edith heard the clink of the gate latch and knew that the caretaker was starting his rounds on the other side of the church. She had only a few minutes to get away before he spotted her.

There was only one thing left that she knew how to do, one way in which she was sure she could make enough money to survive another Christmas. She had to sell evergreens.

She hated it with everything in her heart, but she had no choice. Slowly, stiffly, she got up and shuffled out onto the streets to find evergreens somewhere that she could sell.

~ ~ ~ ~ ~

Edith supposed that the holly bush in the corner of the garden was a beautiful one, if one cared for holly bushes. Its spiky leaves were a perfect shade of green, dotted with brilliant, scarlet berries; among the whites and greys of slumbering London, it was a splash of vibrant colour.

Snow had dusted its leaves and branches. The glimmering snowflakes only lent to its enchanting appearance.

Edith thought its beauty a hopeless extravagance, an audacious imposition on the quiet grieving of the wintry world, but that couldn't matter to her right now. All that mattered was that this holly would sell effortlessly on the streets.

This part of Finsbury was comparatively upmarket; the houses here were not manors, but they had a modest prosperity about them, with freshly painted shutters and meticulous gardens.

Carriages rolled past her, and the pavement was comparatively empty.

The holly bush was growing in one of those neatly kept gardens, the top of it visible over a low garden wall. There was so much of it – it looked a little overgrown, in truth.

Edith inched a little nearer, sweeping her hands once more through her pockets, mostly out of habit. She knew that there was nothing in them.

There was an old man in the garden, by the back door of the house, stiffly shovelling a pathway through the snow.

Edith watched him for a few seconds, trying to guess by the sight of him if he was going to be willing to help her.

He seemed a jolly old fellow; short and portly, with very red cheeks and a crazy mop of white hair that matched his bushy beard. He wore a bright red coat and boots, and he was humming to himself as he shovelled.

He looked like Father Christmas. Edith remembered the stories Mama had told her about Father Christmas, and they gave her a tiny flicker of courage, just enough to raise her voice and call out, "Hello! Excuse me, sir?"

The old man stopped shovelling and looked around, his milky blue eyes resting on her. "Hello, young lady!" he called.

He sounded jovial enough. Edith dared to hope a little. She stepped closer to the fence. "What a beautiful holly bush you have there, sir."

"Thank you kindly! It certainly awakens one's Christmas cheer."

Edith gritted her teeth, hating those words, but she kept her tone sweet. "Oh, yes, sir, it's a pleasure to the eye. Why, I wanted to ask you, sir…" She leaned against the wall, trying not to let her desperation show. "Would you let me have a sprig or two?"

Instantly, the old man's eyes changed. They darkened, narrowing in suspicion as he gripped his spade.

"Please, sir, I'm not asking idly," said Edith quickly. "I lost a few bunches of flowers yesterday, and I have no money left, but if I could sell some holly – I'm a flower-seller, you see, and…"

"Begone with you then, wench!" barked the old man, brandishing his spade.

Edith took a stumbling step back. "Oh, no, sir, I'm not that kind of flower girl!" she cried. "I'm just trying to make an honest living, and I'll pay you back, I swear I will, you can name your price!"

"I told you to leave!" shouted the old man. "Get away from here, you little hussy, you pretentious and insolent child!"

Edith turned and stumbled off, ducking around the corner of another house and peering out from behind it to see what the old man would do next. Shaking his head, he started shovelling again. Edith's heart stung at his words.

What would it matter to him, to sell her just a few sprigs of holly? There was so much holly on that bush. Mercy had been right about rich folk. Neither of them cared one bit for the poor.

She couldn't drag her eyes away from that holly, aware of the hunger that was sapping the strength from her muscles, making them feel like they would shrivel up and disappear.

All she needed was some of that beautiful, hateful holly, that the gullible masses would buy in bunches, and then she would at least have something to eat tonight, even if she didn't know where she would lay her head.

A few fat flakes of snow started to drift down from the grey heavens. They were feathery white, exactly the kind of snow that Edith had loved in the days when she had had shelter from it, but now the sight of them filled her with dread.

Soon the streets would be filled with snowdrifts, and everything would grow even harder for Edith.

The old man had stopped shovelling. He looked up, squinting at the sky, and muttered some more. Then he stumped off into the house, slamming the back door behind him.

Edith was halfway across the street before she even knew what she was doing. For a second, she dithered there on the stones, part of her feeling a wave of guilt. What would Mama have said?

Her heart hardened at the thought of her mother, toughening to hold back the wave of pain that threatened to overwhelm her. Mama wasn't here.

She strode forward, glancing quickly towards the house. The curtains were drawn, the back door was closed, and in a few strides she had reached the door and ducked down beneath the wall.

It was the work of moments to reach the holly bush in the back corner, and it shielded her as she straightened up and reached for its slender boughs. They were supple and green, and it was hard work to break them off, but she did it quickly, snapping four big strong sprigs off the bush.

She tucked the holly close against her body, glanced around one more time. The door was still closed; there was no one in the garden. She had gone unseen. A rush of nervousness gripped her, and suddenly she couldn't bear to duck behind the wall again.

Instead, she made a break for it, running for the other side of the street, and it was a mistake. Her holey shoes slapped loudly on the street – but not loud enough to drown out the voice of the old man.

"Thief!" he roared. "Stop thief!"

Edith's heart leaped into her throat. She redoubled her pace, her breath rushing in her lungs. A piercing whistle split the air as she bolted down the street, and then a sound that chilled her to the bones: the baying of dogs.

She glanced over her shoulder just as the old man swung the garden gate open, and there they were, two muscular foxhounds with snapping teeth and burning eyes, their nails scrabbling on the stone as they lunged after her. Their roaring barks tore the air. Just as their fangs would tear her flesh.

Edith's hands tightened on the holly sprigs as she bolted down the street at her best speed, her eyes searching wildly for a way to escape, but she could not let go of that holly. It was her only lifeline now.

Jarring pain shot up her legs with each step, and her weakness was growing; Edith knew she couldn't run much further. She glanced back as she reached the end of the street, and the dogs were getting closer, their raucous baying filling the air. Swinging hard to the left, Edith pounded on and her eyes found a low wall to her right.

She might just be able to scale it. Her aching legs told her that she had no other choice, and she flung herself towards it. For a horrible moment, her fingernails scrabbled around the top, then she found grip and hauled herself up and over the wall with a gargantuan effort.

She teetered on the top of it, the dogs roared at her feet, and then she was tumbling into a heap of musty straw.

She lay there for a bruised few minutes, holding her breath and listening to the snuffling and yipping of the dogs until they gave up and trotted off. She was in a small stable yard; a few curious hackneys looked at her over their stable doors, and a pig snuffled amiably at her feet. The straw reeked. But she was alive, and when she opened her hands, she saw that somehow she had managed to keep the holly intact.

A brief pang of relief ran through her. She might still be able to eat tonight.

~ ~ ~ ~ ~

Edith's elbow throbbed as she headed towards the nearest market square. Truth be told, everything throbbed; her head pounded, her chest burned after her exertion, and her limbs had a steady, sucking ache to them that seemed to leach all the strength from her muscles.

It was about half an hour's walk to the little market square; a narrow, smoky place that was always dingy even on a warm summer's day, let alone in the midst of the falling snow.

There were Christmas decorations up, even here, and Edith hated the sight of the faded bunting and sagging paper chains hanging over the vendors' stalls where they sold cheap clothes, brown bread, and bunches of vegetables.

She hadn't sold anything here for a while, but she vaguely remembered it from the days that James had been working for Mr. Thompson, and she could only hope that someone there would be interested in a bit of holly.

She found a spot for herself on a corner, trying to keep out of the smoke from the old lady nearby who was cooking a rich-smelling stew in a huge cast-iron pot. The smell of it made her mouth water; she started to ache with hunger all the more. Perhaps she could afford a little, if she sold this holly quickly.

"Christmas! Christmas!" she called out, even though the word tasted like acid on her tongue. "Lovely evergreens for your home! Spread the season's cheer! Evergreens for Christmastime!"

There was a decent crowd moving among the market square this evening, and a few of them glanced Edith's way. She held up the holly, its berries very bright in their dreary surroundings. "Evergreens!" she called out. "Get your beautiful evergreens!"

There was a sudden shout from across the square, making Edith jump. She saw a flash of colour and her eyes found a bent little old figure on the opposite corner: an old woman, with a sagging, morose jaw and bloodshot eyes that glared out at the crowds.

She was holding up a pot of expensive hothouse ditto, their delicate purple petals impossibly pretty in the grey day.

"Fresh flowers for your home!" the old woman croaked, her voice barely audible and as bitter as the look in her eyes. She grabbed a fistful of mistletoe from the cart beside her and held it in the air. "Evergreens for your decorations! Brighten your house this Christmas!"

Edith dithered. But there was no denying that people were starting to look over at her. She could sell all this holly right now and buy a bowl of that beef stew, if she kept trying.

Still, it felt wrong to be hawking her wares so close beside another flower-seller who looked just as desperate to make a living. Edith's heart faltered within her. Besides, what good would it do to try to sell her holly here, with such obvious competition?

She studied the old woman's cart for a little longer. There was no holly in it, she realized. The old woman was watching her morosely, as though challenging her to try to cry her wares again. Her eyes were bitter, but Mercy's eyes had been bitter too. A wave of grief and longing swept over Edith.

Maybe this old lady wasn't as bad as she seemed; Mercy hadn't been.

She decided to cross the road, holding her holly tightly just in case the old woman wanted to make a grab for it, and stopped a few feet short of the old woman's cart.

"Hello!" she said, somehow managing to dredge a little brightness from the tar pit of her heart. "My name is Edith Atkinson."

The woman's glare rested on her. "And what do you want, except to take my business from me?" she snapped. "I've been selling my wares here for year upon year in all weathers, and I won't have some young thing take all that away from me!"

Edith stepped back, taken aback by the woman's tone. "Please, ma'am, I want to work with you, not against you," she said. "I only see that I have holly and you don't, and I don't want any trouble, I just…"

"Well, you've made trouble enough already, you young wretch!" shrieked the old woman.

She made a sudden rush at Edith, her yellow teeth displayed in a grimace of rage. "Get away from here! Go on! Get off this square or I'll scratch your eyes out!"

Edith glanced over the old woman's fragile figure. She didn't seem to be any kind of a physical threat, and Edith realized abruptly that she no longer cared if she was competing against the old woman.

She was hungry and cold, and she knew she could sell this holly with or without the help of some angry flower-seller. She turned and strode back to her corner, desperation making her steps quick and confident. Taking up her spot, she turned to the crowd once again.

"Lovely bright holly!" she shouted, her pure young voice rising above the chaos of the square. "Perfect for wreaths and decorations! Cheer your home with colour!"

The old flower-seller tried again, undeterred. "Ditto! Moss-roses! Violets from the hothouse! Get them while they're fresh!"

"Good evening, young lady," said a quiet voice by Edith. She nearly fainted with relief when she looked over and saw a woman in a housekeeper's uniform standing in front of her, purse in hand. "How much for your holly?" the woman asked.

"Oh – it's – it's three pennies a sprig," said Edith, stuttering out the price. She'd been too hungry to think about it.

"Very well then; I'll take two," said the woman. She gave Edith a sixpence and took the two biggest sprigs, then bustled off as though she hadn't just saved Edith's very life.

She stared down at the coin in her palms, trembling with relief. She could eat tonight.

"Mr. Brooks!" called the croaking old voice of the other flower-seller. "Some mistletoe for you today, sir?"

Edith looked up. A young gentleman had paused on the street beside the old flower-seller, but he glanced over her wares without interest.

They were poor, to be honest; the ditto was pretty, but the mistletoe was missing several leaves, and the moss-roses had wilted.

"Do you have any holly?" the gentleman asked.

The flower-seller sent Edith a venomous look, then shook her head. "I do have beautiful violets, sir! Straight from the hothouse."

"Ah, it's holly I'm looking for. Not today, Mrs. Bell." With that, the gentleman turned around and strode right over to Edith, reaching into his pocket for his wallet. "Is this all the holly you have, girl?"

"Yes, sir," said Edith eagerly.

"I'll take it, then."

"That'll be sixpence."

The young gentleman gave her the money, and Edith felt as though she could cry with relief.

She now had an entire shilling with her, and it would get her a bowl of warm stew and then she could tackle her problems on a full stomach.

She hadn't realized that the old flower-seller had crossed the square towards her until the old woman was almost on top of her, waving her arms wildly, her shock of yellow-brown hair bursting wildly around her face as though her head was exploding. "Go away!" she shrieked again, her voice like the cry of an old raven. "This is my patch. Get off it!"

Edith backed away a few steps, but she was desperate to cling to this spot, and the old woman had angered her.

"I'm done for today," she said, spreading her hands in a non-threatening gesture.

"Yes, in ten minutes!" The old woman spat on the pavement at Edith's feet. "Don't you dare come back here, do you hear me? I'll knock your silly little head off!" She brandished a tiny, skinny fist.

Edith was exhausted, but she also knew that this was the best patch she'd had in months, and that her survival depended on keeping it. "I'm not competing with you," she said stubbornly. "I'm selling holly. You don't have any."

"Oh, but I will have holly tomorrow," growled the old woman. "And you had better not be here, or I'll give you a piece of my mind!"

"Oi, old crone! Shut your trap!"

Edith jumped, and they both looked over towards the old lady with the stewing pot. She was fixing the old flower-seller with an angry, beady-eyed glare. "Leave the girl alone. She's a sight more pleasant to have around than you are, Mrs. Bell," barked the stew lady. "Get back to your corner and stop bothering her!"

"Yeah, leave the girl alone!" chipped in the nearby grocer. "She has as much right to sell her wares here as you do."

The old woman's face turned scarlet. Her mouth worked, as though she was struggling to hold back her words, but she settled for giving Edith a savage glare before spinning around and striding back to her handcart.

"Come over here, deary," said the stew lady. "You look half starved, and I've an extra bowl here for you."

Edith could hardly believe her ears, even a few minutes later, when she sat in the lee of the grocer's stall — he had said she could sleep there — and ate an entire bowl of hot stew for which she'd only paid tuppence. She had more than enough money left to buy some stock for tomorrow. A tiny seedling of hope was beginning to take root in her heart once more.

She could only pray that it would survive this Christmas.

Chapter Thirteen

It felt good to be walking through the city with fresh bunches of cut flowers in her hands again. Edith cuddled the hothouse flowers carefully to her chest, keeping them out of the chilly wind. They were beautiful things. Farringdon's hothouses were not as good as Covent Garden's, but somehow they had managed to bring forth some beautiful white mignonettes. At this time of year, Edith had paid a premium for them; but she would be able to sell them for much more on her new patch.

It had been treating her well for several days now. So well, in fact, that she had finally been able to venture away from selling the holly and mistletoe that she hated so much. She hoped that the mignonettes would do just as well as her evergreens had done.

As she walked onto the square, her senses were assaulted with the coming Christmas. Everywhere she looked, someone had put up little twists of mistletoe with candles in among them; holly wreaths hung from all the stalls, which were also draped in brightly coloured bunting.

The smell of oranges was thick in the air. The man who sold clothes was singing to himself as he packed out his wares.

Deck the halls with boughs of holly...

The words pierced right through Edith's soul, and an aching memory came back to her: standing in the kitchen, baking bread, and singing that same old carol, her voice united with James'.

It had been a long time since she had allowed a thought of James to slip through. Edith gritted her teeth against it, blinking back her tears. She had forgotten James, had pushed him into some dark corner of her mind where she would never have to feel the pain of losing him again.

But it was hard to forget with Christmas all around her. Perhaps that, more than anything else, was what she hated most about this time of year.

She pushed past the stalls and the first few shoppers who had trickled into the marketplace.

The stew lady — a widow named Mrs. Mann — was roasting chestnuts in the fire to sell. Their familiar scent brought back a tide of memories, and Edith had to fight them back, greeting Mrs. Mann's cheerful greeting with a sharp nod as she arranged her flowers in the pail of water at her feet.

"Are you all right today, deary?" Mrs. Mann asked.

Edith met her eyes, forcing back her grief. "Oh, I'm fine."

Mrs. Mann's eyes softened with compassion. "Are you warm enough at night?"

Edith didn't want to tell this sweet little old lady that her current sleeping spot – in the corner by the grocer's stall, with a bit of cardboard for a mattress and two nice thick flour sacks for blankets – was the warmest she'd had all winter.

"Yes, thank you," she said instead.

Mrs. Mann beamed. She had provided one of the flour sacks. "Truth is, dear, we'd be glad to have you here always," she said. "You don't make as much trouble as the Bells."

"The Bells?" Edith echoed. She glanced over at the opposite corner, where the old flower-seller gave her a morose glare while she was packing out her wares.

"I suppose Mrs. Bell isn't so bad," said Mrs. Mann. "She's a grumpy old crone but there's no real harm in her. Customers don't like her, but they don't know what she has to deal with." She snorted. "Mr. Bell, on the other hand – now he's a piece of work if I ever saw one."

"Oh?" said Edith, feeling hairs rise on the back of her neck.

"Yes, he's a real good-for-nothing, that one," scoffed Mrs. Mann. "Hasn't worked a stitch in years, not since he came back from the fighting in Burma; he's more interested in drinkin' and chasin' after younger girls than working to support his poor old wife.

He does bits and bobs of odd jobs, piecemeal like, but he never holds onto anything much for long. Poor old Mrs. Bell has no choice but to work her fingers to the bone trying to support him. Sometimes he comes over here, and that causes nothing but trouble. Scares the customers right off."

Edith watched Mrs. Bell with a wary eye. She felt a tug of sympathy at her heart for the poor old lady, wondering what it must be like to have to support two people – and knowing that one's husband could make one's life much easier, if only he made the effort.

Still, her primary thought was simple. She hoped, with all her heart, that Mr. Bell wouldn't come to the market square while she was here.

But the glowering look Mrs. Bell was giving her suggested that meeting Mr. Bell was growing ever more likely.

~ ~ ~ ~ ~

"Moss-roses!" Edith pitched her voice high, a belling note that had served her well for many of her years on the street. "Yellow and white! Pink and red! Beautiful moss-roses for your study or kitchen! Fresh hothouse moss-roses, only tuppence for a bunch!"

"Cowslips! Pansies! Lily-of-the-valley!" croaked Mrs. Bell, but her reedy old voice was lost in the rush of the crowd that had filled the little market square from edge to edge.

It was a few days before Christmas; everyone was frantically getting ready for their celebrations, and as much as Edith hated the very thought, she was certainly taking advantage of the extra traffic coming through the square.

Right now, a young woman was hurrying towards her, tugging at the buttons on her purse. "Do you have white moss-roses?" she asked breathlessly, her eyes wide with excitement.

"I do," said Edith quickly, lifting a bunch of them from the pail of water at her feet. "Beautifully fragrant too, miss. Tuppence for a bunch; but I'll give you four for sixpence."

"I just need one for now. Thank you." The girl tipped two pennies into Edith's palm, then took the moss-roses and lifted them to her nose. She took a deep breath, a smile lifting her lips. It was snowing softly, and the flakes had settled like stars on her dark eyelashes. "Oh – they smell wonderful."

"Thank you kindly, miss," said Edith. "I have pink ones too, and red and yellow."

"Oh no, thank you," said the girl, giving Edith an enchanting smile. "I only want the white. My mama just loves white moss-roses, and I've wrapped her present with the loveliest white ribbons. These moss-roses will be a perfect decoration."

The young woman walked away, and Edith found herself suddenly tongue-tied and aching deep inside her heart as a memory flooded back to her, as they did so sharply and so intrusively at this time of the year.

When she was about ten or eleven years old, Edith had spoken in secret to all the parents whose children attended the dame-school, asking them to contribute just a penny or even a farthing so that she could buy her mother a present from all of them. They had enthusiastically done so, and Edith had been able to give Mama two books she'd bought second-hand. She would never forget the look of enchantment on Mama's face when she'd opened the parcel on Christmas morning.

It was one of her favourite memories, and that made it sting all the more now. She blinked tears from her eyes, bending down and pretending to busy herself with her flowers.

Why did Christmas always make her remember? All she wanted to do was survive – and forget.

In the corner of her eye, Edith saw a figure heading towards her through the crowd. Swallowing hard, she forced down her tears. She still had many moss-roses to sell if she was going to make enough money in the next few days to carry her through the utter stillness that would be Christmas Day.

Straightening up, she held up a bunch of the yellow moss-roses. "Good morning, sir!" she cried, seeing the old gentleman approaching her; he was a scruffy-looking figure, with a bald patch in the middle of his head and ragged clothes that clung to his scrawny frame, but he was moving towards her with purpose. "A bunch of flowers for your lady wife?" Edith called.

The old man rushed towards her, and Edith only realized that he wasn't slowing down when it was already too late. One of his skinny fists flew through the air towards her, and she ducked just too late; it caught her a glancing blow on the temple that sent pain blooming through her head, and she staggered backwards, tripped over her pail, and landed heavily on her back. Frigid water gushed over her skirts, and her flowers spilled onto the pavement.

"No!" Edith gasped, grasping at them and pulling them close before they could be damaged or trampled.

"Flowers for my lady wife?" cried the old man. "Flowers for my *wife*? My wife has nothing but flowers, you stupid wench – it's you that she needs to be rid of!"

Edith clung to her flowers and looked up at the old man, whose eyes were blazing with anger, his fists bunched where he stood over her. This had to be Mr. Bell.

"Please, sir, I don't want any trouble," Edith stammered. She sat up, grasped her pail and pulled it closer, putting the flowers carefully inside. She had paid all her money for them – losing them would ruin her all over again.

"You don't want any trouble?" cried Mr. Bell. "You don't want any *trouble*?" The words came out on a huff of air that smelled utterly stale, almost fermented. Mr. Bell's eyes were unfocused too, and he swayed a little as he shook a skinny fist at her. "Then you should never have come to my wife's patch, you filthy little wretch!"

"Sir, I have nowhere else to go," cried Edith.

"I don't care!" roared Mr. Bell. "Just go! Go! Take your flowers and leave – before I make you!"

Edith stumbled to her feet, her hip burning where she had fallen, and lifted the pail. Dread clutched at her. Where else could she sell all these moss-roses before they wilted? She truly didn't have anywhere else to go, but she could see a murderous look in Mr. Bell's eye, saw the way the muscles bunched in his thin shoulders as he prepared to take another swing at her –

"What is the meaning of this?" demanded an angry voice.

Edith felt a rush of relief and looked up to see one of her most regular customers. Mr. Stanley always had a flower in his buttonhole; he was wearing one of her red moss-roses right now, and his face was almost the same colour as the little bloom as he glared at Mr. Bell.

"This girl is a thief, guv!" shouted Mr. Bell, his words slurring. "She's a thief!"

Mr. Stanley gave Edith a surprised look.

"I am no thief, sir!" Edith said angrily. "I merely happen to be selling flowers on the same square as Mrs. Bell – I have stolen nothing!"

"Nothing but my wife's business!" roared Mr. Bell, saliva flying on his words. "You've stolen our livelihood, you little hussy, you – "

He lunged at Edith again, but this time Mr. Stanley stepped forward and gave him a hearty shove with the flat of one hand, sending Mr. Bell reeling off almost into the crowd again.

"That's quite enough, you rascal!" said Mr. Stanley sharply. "You leave this young lady alone, do you hear me? Or should I call for the policeman on the street corner?"

The word *policeman* instantly stopped Mr. Bell in his tracks. He glared at Mr. Stanley, saying nothing.

"I thought not," said Mr. Stanley. "Now leave the girl alone, and find yourself something gainful to do, you old drunkard!"

Mr. Bell glowered at him for a moment more, then stumped away, getting lost in the crowd. Edith's shoulders sagged with relief. She turned to Mr. Stanley. "Oh, sir, I – "

"Say nothing of it, young lady," said Mr. Stanley. "Your wares are far better than the old woman's, and you can count on my support always." He winked at her, then strutted off, his bright green top-hat standing out among the crowd.

"I'm so glad Mr. Stanley was here!" cried Mrs. Mann, who had been watching, wide-eyed, from her stall. She shook her head. "The audacity of that old drunkard! Why, he's – he's – I don't even know what to say about him. Are you hurt, deary?"

"No," said Edith, not entirely truthfully. Her head throbbed, and she could feel a bruise growing on her hip. "I'm quite all right."

"Well, I hope you don't listen to a word that old fool says," said Mrs. Mann. "He's nothing but a bag of wind, that's all. You forget about him, deary, and sell your flowers wherever you like. Here – take some water from my kettle for your flowers. I just drew the water; it's not too warm yet."

Edith shakily thanked Mrs. Mann, but she kept glancing over her shoulder at Mrs. Bell. The old flower-seller's eyes were fixed upon her, and there was a burning hatred in them, just as she'd seen in the eyes of Mr. Bell.

She could only hope that Mrs. Mann was right.

~ ~ ~ ~ ~

Even though Edith had hated every moment of hawking holly to the crowds today, she was glad, now, that she had gritted her teeth and done it. The pathetic platitudes and empty well-wishes she'd called out to passers-by had been worth it; she'd sold every scrap of holly she had had left, and at a good price, too.

It seemed that the last few days before Christmas was the time when panicky housewives and housekeepers rushed out looking for evergreens to put the finishing touches on her decorations.

At any rate, Edith now had more money than she could even have dreamed of for a long time.

Enough that she had been able to leave the market and hurry to Farringdon, where the impatient old woman who sold hothouse flowers there had been ready to go home for the holidays and wanting to sell everything she had left as cheaply and quickly as possible.

Edith had bought all the hothouse flowers she had, and she carried them now in two pails of water, determined to keep them fresh until the day after Christmas. Then she could get a head start on selling them when almost no one else would have any.

It wasn't quite contentment that Edith felt as she walked back through the dark streets towards her market square. It was too cold for contentment. The weather was blustery, the stars long retreating behind a thick grey blanket of clouds, fistfuls of cold snow blowing up against Edith's face and nipping at the bare skin of her hands.

She wished for gloves, not for the first time. But if she made it through Christmas Day, she thought, maybe she could even buy some.

Perhaps this Christmas Day would be the exception for her, the day when nothing went horribly wrong. She felt a flicker of hope again, and clung to it.

She might be cold and homeless and desperately poor, it was true; but at least she had the security of knowing that she had money for food for two or three days, and enough flowers to sell after that that she could almost guarantee a week's good eating. It had been a long time since Edith had last known that kind of security.

She allowed herself to let out a long breath, focusing on that fact to keep herself from tumbling into the black abyss of loneliness that was always yawning at her feet. She was going to enjoy the hot soup she'd bought at Farringdon, and then she was going to cuddle down under the extra sacks she'd bought from Mrs. Mann and sleep. Maybe she would even have enough money to make it through Christmas Day, if business was good tomorrow.

The sound of her feet echoed hollowly around the street. It was very late; the lines had been long at Farringdon, and her limbs ached with exhaustion. She doubted that there would be anyone at all left in the market square. The thought filled her with a hollow ache.

The mouth of the market square yawned black and empty in front of her, and she had just enough time to wish she'd thought to buy a candle before it happened.

She felt the blow coming, rather than hearing it, some animal instinct reaching into the pit of her stomach and making her duck just in time. The club that had been viciously aimed towards her head glanced over her shoulder instead with biting pain, and Edith reeled into the street, dropping both pails. Water gushed over the street, freezing almost instantly; her flowers were scattered everywhere, but that was the least of her problems.

When she rolled onto her back, the mad face of Mr. Bell was barely illuminated by a distant streetlamp, but she saw enough to know that he was baying for blood. He swung the club back over his shoulder and took aim again, and Edith rolled desperately, the club thudding into the street with an awful crunch as it splattered some of her flowers into the stone.

She found her feet somehow and stood up, facing Mr. Bell, who was swaying on his feet, the club still in his hands. "Sir, please!" she gasped. Her shoulder ached sharply; she tried to move her arm, but it sent a pang of bitter pain through her body.

"I told you to leave," Mr. Bell hissed.

Edith's heart hammered. She could see death in his eyes, and she had never known such fear. But her flowers... They were all the wealth she had in the world, and they lay all over the street. If she ran from him now, she would lose them.

"I'll go," she stammered. "I'll go, I promise. Only let me pick up my flowers. Please, sir, let me – "

"You witch!" shrieked Mr. Bell, his words taking on an unearthly tone. "I'll kill you. I'll kill you!"

He came after her then, swinging the club in deadly arcs, and Edith backed away as quickly as she could, her eyes still on the flowers. Her heart was crying out that she needed to run and grab them. She had enough money to eat tomorrow, or to buy more stock – but not both...

The club whistled past her face, so close that she felt the wind of it, and she leaped back, feeling pain lance through her hip and shoulder. "I'll kill you!" shrieked Mr. Bell. "I'll kill you!"

"Sir, please, I just need my flowers!" Edith begged, still backing away.

But his eyes were mad, blank with fury, and he was lunging at her with more and more power as though drawing strength from some depth of pain and rage that even Edith couldn't fathom.

They were some way down the street now, and she thought that if she could only feint to the left, then dart to the right, perhaps she could get around him and grab a few of those flowers and her pails before she had to flee.

It was her only hope. Gathering herself, she darted left. Mr. Bell followed, but when she lunged to the right, he was too quick for her, his body remembering its training as a soldier in bygone years. The club hammered into her ribs, throwing her to the ground; she skidded across the icy street, unimaginable pain blooming through her chest.

"I've got you now, you ugly Russian!" howled Mr. Bell.

He had gone mad, had lost himself in his memories of the war, and Edith knew there was no escaping him. Barely able to breathe, she forced herself to her feet. He was still coming at her. She had no choice. Doubled over in agony, she ran away, each step sending fresh waves of pain through her ribs, each step carrying her further away from the momentary security she had so nearly enjoyed.

Chapter Fourteen

Edith woke half-frozen late the next morning. She could remember only bits and pieces of what had happened the night before. Mr. Bell's attack was crystal clear; her flowers spread on the stones, the agony of the blow to her ribs, her rising terror as he screamed out how he was going to kill her. That much she could remember effortlessly.

But after that, everything was a blur. She had fled. Fled as fast as her feet would carry her, with Mr. Bell ever in pursuit, with her shoulder and ribs hurting more with each stride. Somehow Mr. Bell had kept up with her even in his stupor, and his shrieks had chased her through the city; there had been not a soul on the street to hear her cries for help. They were all locked inside behind decorated doors, in the golden rooms filled with candlelight, heedless of the hardship that continued just outside their snug little worlds.

Eventually, she had lost him, but the fear of him had continued to hunt her through the streets until she finally could run no further.

It was sheer, dumb luck that had led her to the sheltered spot where she'd been sleeping ever since: a corner between two buildings and what looked like a market stall. Edith hadn't cared what it was last night. She'd only cared about getting out of the wind, and she had collapsed there and slept.

Part of her had nearly hoped that the cold would take her peacefully during the night. Instead, she woke to sunshine on her face. There was no wind, and almost no sound at all; just occasional bursts of laughter and singing from the street on the other side of the stall. Mercifully, the stall itself remained unoccupied. Was it Christmas Eve today? It had to be. Clearly, no one would be selling anything today.

Edith could only pray that she might.

She blinked painfully against the sun. Her shoulder was aching, true, but far worse was the pain in her ribs. When she lay on her injured side they were strangely a little better; she could breathe tolerably well like that. But if she moved, they sent stabs of absolute agony knifing through her body, so that it was all she could do not to scream in pain.

She reached into her pocket, her movements slow and inching against the pain, and pulled out the money she had kept for food. It had felt like a fortune last night, but that was when she had had stock for four days or more. Now, it was barely enough to buy one of two things: a few bunches of hothouse flowers, or a square meal.

She couldn't buy both.

Edith let her head bump onto the ground again, her arm flopping limply onto the cold stone, and felt the tears filling her eyes.

Even if she bought stock instead of food, where would she sell it? There would be no going back to the corner by Mrs. Mann's, that much was certain. And she had tried everywhere else. Every market, every corner, every cemetery... she didn't know of anywhere that was left.

Christmas had robbed her of all hope yet again.

She gritted her teeth, forcing back her tears, and tried to do as she always did when the pain threatened to overwhelm her; she tried to think practically. What could she do right now to stay alive? She could buy food, but that would condemn her to starvation, with no other choice but to steal in order to buy flowers again. Stealing was risky, as she'd discovered with the holly. She wasn't going to try that again.

Maybe she would be lucky and find some hopeless vendor with a few flowers left for her to purchase this afternoon, and if she was very lucky, she might be able to sell them before the Christmas Eve festivities began.

The familiar old ache of hunger in her belly was bad enough, but when she tried to rise, the stinging pain in her ribs was far worse. It took her several minutes just to get to her feet, keeping one arm clamped to her chest and taking slow sips of air when she was able. Tears were running down her cheeks when she finally straightened a little and managed to take a few steps forward.

She pushed the thought from her mind and stepped out from behind the market stall, and instantly froze to the spot. Everything around her was familiar, utterly familiar, even though she hadn't seen this market square for years.

She could never forget a single detail of the scene before her. It was branded into her memory with a blazing rod of iron.

She knew it all: the snow-dusted shops with their bunting and bright wreaths, from the pawn shop where she'd bought those books for Mama to the bakery that had always sold them her Christmas treat; the jingle of bells as carriages moved through the square, bursts of laughter coming from their windows; the snow that glittered in soft powder on every surface, like so many tiny diamonds in the gentle winter sunlight; the great Christmas tree in the centre, towering over it all, its star glimmering at the top, the white candy canes and ribbons hanging from every bough.

A sob tore through Edith's body, wrenching her ribs. She sank to the ground, unnoticed, and stared at the tree with its many red ribbons.

This was the square where Mama had been killed six years ago today.

Edith buried her face in her hands and sobbed for everything she had lost, sobbed for the twelve-year-old girl who had walked through this square six years ago not knowing that the whole world would soon be torn away from her, sobbed for little Donna and the hardship the poor child had had to endure, sobbed for James and what would never be between them.

But most of all, she sobbed for Mama, for that radiant life so cruelly and abruptly snuffed out, and she wept with all of her heart because of the emptiness that Mama had left in her soul. In that moment she could no longer be angry with Christmas anymore.

She wanted, more than anything, to believe in it the way she once had done. But when she searched her heart for the ability to have faith again, it was gone.

It was too late for her. She was empty, wrung out of all belief, stripped of everything but her desire to survive, and even that was waning now in the face of her constant agony.

She was still weeping when a bunch of carollers came past. They were singing "God Rest Ye Merry Gentlemen", and the words felt like knives on Edith's soul. Each was carrying a little bouquet of flowers, nothing like the cheap ones that Edith bought and sold, but beautiful, fresh, vivid things straight from the most expensive hothouses in London. They had come, no doubt, from the popular florist on the corner, which had been there for years: another reason why she had never been back to this market square to try to sell flowers.

Edith stared at them, knowing that with just one of those bouquets, she could make enough money to survive for several days. The carollers passed by, and Edith let out a sigh of dismay. Those flowers would be cast aside at the end of the night as if they were nothing.

Edith knew how that felt.

She turned her eyes to the florist's shop. Maybe, just maybe, there would be a few flowers thrown out on their rubbish pile that she could salvage. If they were only a little wilted, someone might still want them tonight.

Clutching her ribs, trying to ignore the fiery pain in her shoulder, and plodded towards the shop. It was just another desperate, desolate Christmas Eve.

~ ~ ~ ~ ~

It turned out that the florist had been wasteful. It had closed already, and Edith could root through the rubbish undisturbed. Like the flower vendor at Farringdon, they had had extra flowers to get rid of that would have wilted during Christmas Day; but thanks in part to the cold, some of them were still quite respectable. Edith was able to scrounge a few, which left her with a few pennies to buy food.

The baker sold her a heel of stale bread as he was closing up his shop, not recognizing her at all. At least she had managed to find some bits of fairly dry wood to make a fire, and melted some snow over it, putting her flowers in a tin cup she'd pinched from the florist's rubbish. They would be all right until tomorrow, but then where would she shell them?

This market square was hopeless with the florist right there; all the squares in walking distance, Edith had already tried, and been chased off by jealous root-sellers or the police, suspecting that she was a different kind of flower girl.

She had even tried selling at all the cemeteries in walking distance that she knew of. All of them except for one.

A tear coursed down her cheek, its brief warmth bringing scant comfort to her skin even as it shattered her heart. She had no choice now.

She would have to go to the cemetery where Mama was buried.

~ ~ ~ ~ ~

Edith reached the cemetery just as the afternoon was turning into evening.

It was a scant hope that anyone would be along to buy flowers today, but the bobby on the corner of the market square she had once loved was starting to give her suspicious looks, and she'd known that she had to leave. So even though it was the last place on Earth she ever wanted to be, Edith was now walking up to that same cemetery.

It was just as she remembered it. The little stone church on the other side of the property, its windows glowing golden as the Christmas Eve sermon was prepared.

The handful of gravestones scattered across the lumpy ground. A few weary little trees, bent and twisted as they clung to life in the hard earth, their branches bare in the afternoon sunlight.

For all that the sun was, unusually, shining, it was bitterly cold. Edith had planned to stand at the cemetery gate, to not even look over at the place where Mama was buried. She could hardly remember where exactly the grave had been.

But when she reached the gate, her feet wouldn't stop. She was drawn as if by an invisible force into that graveyard, as though she might find her mother there somehow, right where she had left her.

The gate swung behind her with a hollow, rattling sound that made Edith think of bones for some reason. She brought the tin cup of flowers with her, loathe to let them out of her sight, and wandered among the graves.

There were not many, and most of them were unkempt and neglected. The stones were chipped and cracked, and there were no footprints through the snow except Edith's.

One gravestone, however, still looked new and clean, even polished. It caught her eye. It couldn't be Mama's, of course. No one had been to her grave in years – except that they had: when Edith drew nearer, she saw the name on the gravestone and it stopped her heart in her chest.

Susan Atkinson, Beloved Mother. She is clothed in strength and dignity; she laughs without fear of the future.

The quote seemed Biblical, and Edith knew she should know it, but now all that she could think of was that she hadn't read her mother's name in almost six years.

The sight made Mama's name echo through her mind, *Susan*, its sibilant quality in her imagination filling her eyes with tears. How she missed hearing that name! How she missed hearing the parents say it in tones of deep gratitude every evening! How she missed hearing James say *Mrs. Atkinson* with reverence and respect!

There were so many other things she missed about Mama. She stood in front of the grave, reading the name over and over until her eyes blurred with tears and dripped down her cheeks, and for the first time she allowed herself to lean into her memories, into how much she missed her mother.

She missed the sound of Mama's breath in the early mornings before either of them was fully awake. She missed the hoarseness of her voice before she had had her morning tea. She missed her laughter and her smile as Mama worked with the children.

She missed the tiny wrinkle that appeared above each eyebrow when Mama was really enjoying her book.

She missed the way Mama would tickle her when she was sad, and the way Mama would hug her every single morning at breakfast, and the way Mama said "I love you" and even the way Mama yelled when she was angry and the way she made the porridge rather too dry every morning. —and her footsteps in the hallway and her presence in the room and the indefinable magic that always seemed to glow in her eyes...

Mama had been the Christmas magic for Edith. But she wasn't here. She was gone.

Edith fell to her knees in the snow, simply staring at Mama's beautifully polished gravestone. She closed her eyes tightly, sending tears coursing down her cheeks.

The memories were flooding over her now, and they all burned, but somehow it was a good pain. It was good to let herself remember at last, and even to let herself imagine that Mama was right here beside her.

She flinched over the thought at first, realizing how far away she was from the future that Mama had dreamed for her.

But when she truly took the time to imagine her mother's presence, she could see the love sparkling in her eyes, hear the depth of compassion in her voice. Mama had never judged anyone.

She had only shown people love, and she knew, suddenly and completely, that if Mama was here, she would be kind. "Everything will be all right," she'd say. "Just keep believing, Edie."

She could almost hear those words ringing through her mind.

Fresh tears gushed down her cheeks, but this time, there was gratitude in them. All this time, she had been trying to forget that Mama even existed, when the truth was that perhaps a piece of Mama was still alive: her unshakable love was still burning brightly, deep inside Edith's spirit.

Perhaps it was enough to get her through one more Christmas. Enough to help her believe a little.

~ ~ ~ ~ ~

Sunny Christmas Eve had given away to one of the most bitterly cold days Edith had ever known. She stood shivering at the gate to the cemetery, blowing on her hands from time to time and praying that the water in her tin cup wouldn't freeze. She kept swirling it a bit, in a bid to keep it liquid.

The flowers still looked all right, for now, and she'd tried to arrange them into two tasteful little bunches. Maybe someone would buy them. Maybe someone, somewhere in London, wanted to visit this cemetery today.

There were a few people passing by, and Edith wondered how none of them were freezing. They were bundled up, to be sure, with coats and hats and scarves, but no one seemed to be feeling the viciousness of the cold that she was.

She didn't think she'd ever been this cold before. It felt as though her very bones had turned into ice, and she just couldn't stop shivering, making the water slosh and rattle in the tin cup.

Her head throbbed. Somewhere inside it, distantly, she knew that she was sick. But what could she do about it? She needed food, and to get food, she needed to sell these flowers.

That was all she could think of now; that and the terrible cold, and the fact that with every shudder that wracked her spine, a fresh wave of utter agony washed through her body.

With chattering teeth, she wondered if she should try crying her wares a little. Clearly, no one was interested in this cemetery, even if Edith's whole world lay buried there. People might think her odd, selling flowers at a cemetery gate, but what did that matter as long as they paid her?

"Flowers," she whispered. Her voice wouldn't call out. "Flowers for the poor." No, wait. That didn't sound right. It was *Alms for the poor*. "Lovely flowers," she breathed, but her voice was just too weak. She wanted to take a step forward, but she feared she might collapse where she stood.

She knew all this through a strange kind of veil, as though her suffering had abruptly been separated from her identity. Some part of her was admiring the glittering snow today, enjoying the distant music coming from the church as the congregation sang their Christmas hymns.

The world was beautiful after all. She had had to visit Mama's grave again to realize that, and it saddened her that it had taken her so long to do it. But perhaps her life truly was waning. Perhaps she would soon be in Mama's arms again...

A carriage came rattling to a halt, incredibly, just opposite the cemetery gate. Edith's head yanked up. She stared as the door opened and a tall young gentleman stepped out, followed by a girl who looked to be about eleven.

The girls delicate features promised the potential to become a luminous beauty, with the biggest, most expressive eyes Edith had ever seen – or maybe that was another fever dream.

Either way, taking hands, the two of them began to walk towards her, and Edith quickly dropped her eyes and assumed the reverential attitude that had served her well at cemetery gates before.

"Good morning, sir," she murmured softly, holding up the tin cup. "A flower for your loved one's grave?"

"Oh – how wonderful," said the girl. She had a sweet, belling voice that soothed Edith somehow. "We'd forgotten to bring flowers for Mrs. Atkinson. And it's Christmas Day, too."

"How much are your flowers?" asked the tall young gentleman.

It was only when he spoke that the familiarity of him pierced the fog of Edith's mind. She raised her head slowly, her gaze resting first on the girl, on those gigantic dark eyes of hers, eyes that held all the secrets of the universe.

Then she looked up, and up again. He had grown so much, but the hair was the same, still straw-coloured, still messy despite the neat suit and hat he wore. And the air of utter gentleness still hung around him; in the way he held his wallet, the questioning look in his soft eyes, the beautiful sorrow of the half-smile touching the corner of his mouth.

The tin cup tumbled from her numb fingers, flowers scattered on the snow. She didn't care.

There was such a thing as miracles, after all. Mama had brought back the Christmas magic.

"James?" she breathed.

His eyes widened as they met hers, and she saw him recognize her at once. He took a step towards her, joy and terror clashing in his face.

"Edith!" James cried.

He held out his arms just in time. Edith's knees gave way, and she fell headlong, straight into his arms.

~ ~ ~ ~ ~

They clung to one another in front of that cemetery gate and wept for what seemed to be a lifetime, but it was a good kind of weeping, a cleansing kind, as though Edith's tears were washing away the filth and sorrow that had clouded her soul. She couldn't let James go, her grubby hands locked on the front of his coat; his arms were wrapped around her, hugging him against his frame, which was stronger than it used to be, more fleshed out.

But he still smelt the way he had always smelt — a little cleaner perhaps, but still retaining that essence that was so uniquely his own. Edith buried her face in it, breathed it in huge, sobbing gasps. It told her that this was real. It told her that she had her Christmas miracle at last.

Eventually, she allowed herself to lift her face to his, and James cupped her cheeks in his hands and gazed into her eyes. "Oh, Edie," he breathed.

No one had called her that in three years. The sound of her nickname sent a fresh burst of tears down her cheeks. "I looked for you," she croaked.

"And we looked for you. Everywhere!" said Donna. She seized one of Edith's hands, clinging to it as though she would never let go. "Oh, I can't believe we found you at last."

Her words were so crisp, so educated. Edith stared up at James. "Where have you been?" she breathed.

"We didn't last long in the workhouse." James shook his head, allowing his hands to slide down to her arms. "That spring, the workhouse sold me to a manor house to help the old gardener. I loved the work; we were outside all day, with flowers and plants, but Donna... I had to get Donna back. I visited her as often as I could, but I could see her wasting away."

Donna shuddered, as did Edith. The thought was appalling.

"I didn't earn any money; just my board and lodge. But that changed when the head gardener died. He had recommended me to the owners of the house, and they promoted me to a paid assistant for the new head gardener. As soon as I had enough money, I brought Donna with me and put her back into school."

"Oh, Donna!" Edith cried. The words made her ribs sting, but it was glorious to know that her education had continued after all.

"That was two years ago. Last year, I was given a promotion." James' eyes gleamed. "I'm the head gardener now, and I make a good bit of money, and so we travel here every Sunday and every holiday to pay our respects to your mama... and in the hope of finding you. When our searches were unfruitful, we thought you might come back to your mother's grave."

"I moved away from the workhouse two years ago," said Edith. "That's why you could never find me."

"We searched, Edie. You have to believe that we searched." James' eyes filled with tears. "The thought of you out here, alone… oh, Edie, you poor, poor soul."

Donna squeezed Edith's hand. "She looks sick, Jimmy."

"Of course! What am I thinking?" James took Edith's hand. "Come. You must come home to our cottage on the manor grounds."

A cottage. Home. With James and Donna. It all left her reeling. It was almost too beautiful to be true, but Edith knew it was true, because Mama had been right: there really was goodness and hope in the world. There really was magic and beauty in Christmas, not because there was no pain, but because these good things shone all the brighter for the sadness that surrounded them.

"Yes. Yes please," she breathed. "Please take me home."

She took a staggering step forward, but her limbs wouldn't respond, and she nearly fell. But James was there. He scooped her into his arms, cradling her effortlessly against his broad chest. Donna ran ahead, hailing a cab.

Edith was going home.

Epilogue

Three Years Later
1884

Edith stepped back, eyeing the front of the house as she bit her lip. "Do you think it's a little too much, or should we add more holly?" she asked.

Beside her, Donna put a hand on her hip, arching a delicate eyebrow and pursing her perfect lips. Edith could see why James had been threatening to buy a big dog to keep all the suitors at bay. If only those suitors knew that Donna was planning to become a nurse, and that her studies were her consuming passion, not the prospect of marriage.

She gave Edith a playful glance, and together they studied the front of the house for a few moments longer. It was snowing: huge, fluffy white flakes that poured down from the sky, glittering as they fell in picturesque lines along the roof of the house and on the pavement. Golden candlelight poured from the kitchen window onto the snow.

The window itself was almost obscured with Christmas cards and brightly coloured paper chains. Bunting hung across the front of the house, which was draped in so much holly and mistletoe and wreaths and ribbons that it was almost impossible to see the brick at all.

"I think we need *much* more holly," Donna proclaimed.

Edith laughed. Their house was already the most extravagantly decorated on the whole street, but she loved it that way. "Let's do it!" she said.

They stepped into the kitchen and started cutting neat bits of holly from the boughs on the kitchen table. Edith sighed with contentment, feeling the warmth of the hearth. "I can't believe that this place was in ruins just a few years ago," she said.

Donna smiled. "Now it looks even better than it ever did when it was still a dame school," she said.

Moving back into Mama's house had been easy enough. Mr. Wilkes had succeeded in keeping prying eyes away from it; as soon as Edith came of age it had become her legal property, and so they had simply returned. The florist shop in that same market square with the great Christmas tree had quickly hired Edith, and together with James' income, they had been able to repair the house.

Now, it was even more beautifully decorated than it had been in Mama's time. Through the open door, Edith could just glimpse the Christmas tree standing in the living room. They would play charades tonight, and James was bringing a roast goose back from the market.

Heading back outside, Edith and Donna started covering every open space with sprigs of holly, the beautiful berries as bright as red jewels against the snowy day. They stepped back to admire their work. The house had become a beacon of light in their street, calling all who beheld it to hope in the wonder of Christmastime.

A sweet pang of longing ran through Edith's heart. She wished Mama was here to see this. Mama would have loved everything about this day. Pressing a hand to her chest, she let out a little sigh.

Donna rested a hand on her shoulder. "I miss her, too," she murmured.

"We always will," said Edith. "But it feels as though our hope is even stronger now, having endured what it did."

"You're right," said Donna. She looked over at Edith, a smile hand in hand with the sorrow in her eyes. "Christmas is more than just merry. It's heart-breaking too, but that doesn't mean it isn't beautiful."

"Well, look at this!" cried a cheerful voice. "Isn't this the most beautiful little house in all London?"

"Jim!" Edith wheeled around, her heart glowing as James came striding down the street towards her. He was grinning, his hat and his smile both cocked at a jaunty angle, with a promising parcel tucked under his arm.

"I found us the finest goose you've ever seen," said James. "We're going to have a feast tonight, my love."

He wrapped an arm around her waist and pulled her against him. She wrapped her arms around his neck, giggling a little at his touch. It still made her giddy, even after years.

"I say," said Donna. "That's a little inappropriate, here in the middle of the street."

"No one's watching, Donnie," said James fondly. "Besides, can't a man give his wife a little kiss?"

He leaned down and gave Edith a passionate kiss that scattered goosebumps on her skin. She leaned into him, holding him a little bit closer, overflowing with gratitude for all that her life had become.

"Stop it!" Donna laughed, her voice rich with embarrassment. "Come on. We've still got to go and take all that soup we've been making to Edith's flower girls."

Edith stepped back, beaming up at James. "Thank you for helping me with that," she said gently. "Those girls have come to rely on us for a hot meal on Christmas Eve."

"No one should go hungry at Christmas," said James. "After all, it's the most wonderful time of the year."

Edith leaned against him, closing her eyes for a moment, feeling the power of the season coursing through her veins.

"Yes," she said truthfully. "Yes it is."

Join my Newsletter

And receive a free book

Claim The Beggar Urchins Here